REVENGE OF THE SWEET SIXTEEN KILLER!

BY: SCOTT LEBLANC

Published by:
Light Switch Press
PO Box 272847
Fort Collins, CO 80527

Copyright © 2022
ISBN: 978-1-953284-90-7
Printed in the United States of America

No part of this publication may be reproduced, stored in a retrieval system, or transmitted in any form or by any means – electronic, mechanical, digital photocopy, recording, or any other without the prior permission of the author.

All rights reserved solely by the author. The author guarantees all contents are original and do not infringe upon the legal rights of any other person or work. The views expressed in this book are not necessarily those of the publisher.

CHAPTER 1

SEPTEMBER 17ᵀᴴ, 2027

Rebecca Watson stood silently over the grave of the great uncle she never knew. Scott was killed on his 16th birthday, September 17th, 1981. Although Rebecca never knew her great uncle, her grandfather told her enough stories about him that she practically knew him. Rebecca stood there and said a prayer out loud.

"Lord, please keep my great uncle and grandfather safe by your side. Amen"! Rebecca bent over and laid flowers on her great uncle's grave. She then walked a few feet over and placed flowers on her grandfather's grave. Rebecca then blew a kiss to her grandfather and walked towards her car. As she opened the door to her brand new deep blue convertible, she turned around slowly to take a last look at her grandfather's and great uncle's grave. "Well guys, I won't be seeing you for a while, I'm on my way to Fort Lauderdale." Rebecca turned around and sat in her car and started the engine and drove away.

Rebecca was a beautiful woman with long golden blond hair, ocean blue eyes, and a slender body and stood 5 feet 10 inches. Her smile was stunning and every time she walked into a room, people just adored her. Rebecca was married to Tommy Watson, her high school sweet heart. They were married right after graduation and were happy together for a short period of time. Rebecca never seen the dark side of Tommy and she soon divorced him.

Rebecca had to get out of the town she lived in for over 26 years. The city of Lynn was falling apart in her eyes. She never was the same after her grandfather caught the worst serial killer in the city's history. However, the killer was found not guilty on 34 counts of first degree murders and walked away a free man. Rebecca being only 16 was thrown into the spot light after the trial of Dr. Peter Monteiro. According to her grandfather, Dr. Monteiro threatened to kill her. Dr. Monteiro killed 34 boys and girls on their 16th birthday and his trial ended on her 16th birthday. News media was all over the story. Headlines read 'Granddaughter of Detective Life Threatened', 'The Sweet Sixteen Killer out to Get Detective's granddaughter'. Rebecca couldn't sleep after the trial since she thought she would be killed like all the other kids, until that bloody, sunny day on June 26, 2017.

That day started out like every other summer day for a child who just got out of school for summer vacation. Rebecca woke up and wanted to make the day last forever. Rebecca always woke up early since the trial. She had nightmares continuously since Dr. Monteiro was released, but she always went on with her life like nothing had happened. She thought to herself that she was way too young to let her emotions get in the way of her being a teenager.

Rebecca got dressed and headed to the kitchen. Her grandfather had already left for work that day. She kissed her grandmother on the cheek. Rebecca's grandmother was busy in the kitchen making breakfast. The aroma of bacon filled the house. Rebecca loved bacon with her breakfast, and she loved how her grandmother cooked it just right. Rebecca sat at the table and her grandmother asked "how would you like your eggs dear"? Rebecca replied "May I please have them scrambled today"? Rebecca's grandmother smiled at her and nodded yes and continued to cook the perfect breakfast for her granddaughter.

Rebecca was staying at her grandparents' house for the summer. She loved staying with them since both Grammy and Gramps spoiled her rotten. Whatever she wanted, Rebecca got. Her parents weren't thrilled about it either since both of them was unable to provide as much for her like her grandparents' did. I guess you could say that Rebecca's parents were jealous that they just didn't have the money. Her parents provide the essentials, food, clothing, roof over her head, and of course, private schooling. The private schooling took a toll on Rebecca's parents. But ever since the incident, they pulled her out of school and put her into home schooling with a tutor. Her parents knew she was safe at home, but Rebecca felt like a prisoner. She missed her friends at school and now that it was summer and the news media simmered down, she was now able to hang out with her friends during summer vacation.

After breakfast Rebecca thanked her grandmother and headed out the door to go to the Peabody Mall with her friends. "Bye gram, I'll be home before diner" Rebecca yelled to her grandmother as she fled the house in a hurry, and before her grandmother could say 'Bye', Rebecca was already gone.

Rebecca left the house and headed to the bus stop. She waited for about 15 minutes and the bus still hadn't shown up. "Fuck this shit"! Rebecca said out loud throwing her hands in the air. "I'd be better off walking". As Rebecca turned around to walk the bus finally arrived. Rebecca entered the bus and paid her fare. She took a seat at the back of the bus and she gazed out the window thinking to herself how lucky she is to be alive and to be loved by many.

The bus stopped right in front of the Peabody Mall entrance. The mall was a high end with stores like Macy's, Bloomingdales, and Neiman Marcus. Rebecca loved the mall and she loved hanging with her best friend Maggie. Rebecca knew Maggie since the first grade and have been besties ever since. They both like to shop, gossip, and gawk at boys. Maggie Martin was odd looking. Her hair was black that she tied into pig tails; she had dark brown eyes and wore the most outrages horned rimmed glasses that only a grandmother would wear. Maggie was shorter than Rebecca and only stood 5 feet 4 inches. She wasn't fat, but being small she looked heavier than most. Her face was littered with freckles and she wore braces to straighten her crocked teeth. Maggie was a good girl and she too loved to hang out with Rebecca as much as possible. Rebecca heard someone calling her name.

"Hey Beck, over here"! Maggie yelled.

Rebecca turned around to see Maggie wearing a bright yellow cardigan that covered a black t-shirt and neon pink shorts. Her high top sneakers were just as loud as her clothing with a psychedelic patterned that swirled like the painting Starry Night by Vincent van Gogh. Maggie loved to stand out in a crowd and Rebecca was far more conservative than her. Rebecca wore a normal pair of black Nike sneakers with Levi jeans that were strategically ripped in the knees and t-shirt what was lite blue that complimented her eyes.

Rebecca yelled back to Maggie "bitch, it's about time you got your ass here"!

Rebecca loved to joke around with Maggie and tease the living shit out of her. But as much as Rebecca gave, so did Maggie.

"There's a huge sale going on at Macy's we got to check it out!" Maggie had an excitement in her voice.

"Cool! I need to look at some dresses for a wedding I have to go too." Rebecca replied while rolling her eyes. "I hate going to family shit, and yet I'm still dragged to these things."

Rebecca and Maggie walked into the mall. Soft rock played over the loud speakers as they headed towards Macy's. "So what are you looking to buy Maggie?"

Maggie stopped and had to think "I got no frigging clue." Both of them started to laugh out loud and the strangers walking by looked at them weirdly. "I definitely want to check out the shorts" Maggie said. "I heard they have a new line by Santiago, I love his line of fashion."

As both girls were walking to Macy's, Rebecca had a strange feeling come over her. Something in her mind just didn't seem right. Rebecca always had a 6th sense and usually her premonitions were accurate. Though she didn't know exactly what was going to happen, she knew something was going to happen. Maggie always teased her about it and use to say 'I see dead people' referring to the movie The Sixth Sense.

The mall was unusually crowded for this time of day. A lot of the people looked like high school kids killing time. Rebecca and Maggie arrived at Macy's when Rebecca heard her name being called.

"Rebecca! Rebecca" yelled a strange man she didn't know.

"Who is that Beck?" Maggie asked as she looked towards the stranger.

"He's probably a fucking reporter. Let's go, I don't want to speak with anyone right now."

As they started to walk into the store they heard loud firecrackers go off. The people in the mall started to scramble in all directions. That's when Rebecca knew the sound she heard wasn't a firecracker at all, but actually shots from a gun. Maggie and Rebecca started to run to the store, but the grates were closing due to the active shooter. They decided to make a run for it as the gun fire was coming from the stranger that called Rebecca's name. Maggie and Rebecca both hid behind a new car that was being displayed at the mall. They both crawled under the car as more gun fire went off. People were dropping like flies. Blood was being splattered everywhere in the mall. The screams from the people were deafening. But through all the screaming and gun fire, Rebecca heard the assailant.

"Come out, come out where ever you are Rebecca" said the stranger. "I got a little surprise for you!" The stranger kept shooting at random people. Some were shot in the head, and some were shot in the back as they were running. The amount of ammunition this guy had was unbelievable. He had clips after clips of ammunition. "Come on you little bitch, where the fuck are you hiding?" Rebecca turned to Maggie to see a blank look on her face. She looked down to see she was lying in a puddle of blood. Maggie had been shot and wasn't moving. She knew her best friend was killed.

Rebecca looked to see if the shooter was gone. Where she and Maggie took cover under the car, it was hard to see anything. Rebecca laid quietly until she felt a hand grab her foot. The shooter dragged Rebecca out from under the car as a trail of Maggie's blood followed like a wet mop across the floor. Rebecca started to scream for help at the top of her lungs until she felt the cold metal of the gun barrel next to her head. "Get off the fucking floor you fucking bitch!" The guy grabbed her by the collar and lifted her off the floor onto her feet. Rebecca could now see the entire carnage that just occurred. Bodies were littered everywhere, lifeless bloodied bodies. Rebecca started to sob uncontrollably. "Look around pretty girl, look what's instore for you" the stranger said with a smile. "I wanted to kill you back in April on your 16th birthday, but your grandfather wouldn't let me. Better late than never they say!" Rebecca knew just at that moment that the man with the gun was none other than Dr. Peter Monteiro. Rebecca knew it wouldn't take him long to kill her. He set out for revenge and he didn't want anything to interfere with his job. He didn't care who he took out as long as he reached his trophy. Rebecca was that trophy, the head of the granddaughter of the detective that brought him down. Even though he was found not guilty, his entire career was over because of the trial. Dr. Monteiro grabbed Rebecca by the hair, "look at it bitch! Look what you made me do to get to you! This wouldn't have happened if you just turned around to talk with me. You would have been the only one with blood on the floor, not all these people. Are you happy with yourself?"

A tear ran down Rebecca's face as she knew her time on this earth would be over soon. She did feel terrible about all the innocent people that lost their lives on account of her. But Rebecca wasn't going down easily; she had one last fight in her. Rebecca turned around slowly to see her killer face to face. "Pull the fucking trigger now you son of a bitch!" Rebecca then lifter her knee and hit Peter in the groin so hard you could almost hear his testicles burst. Peter fell to the ground in agony as Rebecca started to run. Peter pulled the trigger aimed at her and he fired his weapon. The bullet hit Rebecca in the back. The hot lead burnt her insides as she stumbled to the ground. Blood was pouring out of her chest where the bullet made its exit. Peter pulled the trigger again, this time hitting her in the back of her left calf. Rebecca screamed in agony. She looked up to see Dr. Monteiro walking towards her. He stopped just inches away.

"Are you ready to die now bitch?" The doctor said with a grin only the Grinch could appreciate. Rebecca closed her eyes and the last thing she heard was the pop of the gun, and everything went black.

Rebecca shook her head to refocus on her driving. She wanted to forget that day that her best friend was killed along with her grandfather who was there to kill Dr. Peter Monteiro. Both her grandfather and Dr. Monteiro both pulled their triggers at the same time hitting each other dead center in the head. Her grandfather died that day saving her life. Rebecca was ever so grateful for the sacrifice her grandfather made that day. But now was the time to leave everything behind. It was time to start a new life in Fort Lauderdale and never look back. It took 10 years to get over the loss of grandfather and best friend Maggie, but she knew they wouldn't want her to sit around and be sad the rest of her life because of one deranged man. Rebecca took a deep breathe, and smiled as she drove on I-95 south to Florida.

CHAPTER 2

A NEW CHAPTER IN LIFE.

Rebecca arrived at her new fully furnished condo in Fort Lauderdale. Her new boss bought her the condo on Las Olas Boulevard, a hip part of town. Her unit was on the 30th floor and had spectacular views of the city and ocean. Rebecca was one of the top criminal profilers in the country. She had a degree from Harvard University for psychology and criminal profiling. Rebecca just landed a job at Thorton Associates, the biggest private criminal profiling firm in the states. The firm was bigger than the Federal Bureau of Investigation's unit. Rebecca couldn't refuse the offer that the firm gave her. She was going to make over 500k a year. She knew looking at the condo that it was expensive, and was impressed that Mr. Thorton bought it for her as a sign on bonus.

Thorton Associates worked with police departments all around the world, profiling criminals and helping the police catch the suspect or suspects of horrific crimes. Though Rebecca was traumatized by Dr. Monteiro, she always wondered what made him tick. After graduating high school as valedictorian, she received a fully paid scholarship to Harvard University where she graduated once again as valedictorian at Harvard.

Rebecca worked with the F.B.I. as a profiler in their Boston office. She flew around the country, checking out the crime scene and making a profile for each and every case. Her track record was unmatched by anyone at the bureau. She had a 98% accuracy rate, the highest rate the F.B.I ever had in the agency.

Though she loved working with the F.B.I, she needed more. She was only 26 and she wanted to see the world, and Thorton Associates were international, not just in the United States. Rebecca could be flying to any country at a moment's notice. Thorton Associates had multiple private jet s that was ready to fly anywhere they were needed.

Rebecca did extensive research on the company before she made her decision to leave the F.B.I. and go to a private firm. Thorton Associates was owned and operated by its founder, Willard P. Thorton. Willard was on the Forbes list of the 100 richest men in the United States, placing him at number 35 with a net worth of 4.5 billion dollars. He started the company after graduating top of his class at Brown University. He studied law and psychology and passed his bar exam in 2006. He worked for a major law firm and quit, since he wanted to catch the criminals he was representing. He didn't like being a defense lawyer winning his cases. He knew that most of his clients were guilty as charged, and that always bothered him, so he went off on his own and started the firm back in 2018. His firm rapidly grew to a multi-billion dollar enterprise in just 2 years. Rebecca was excited that she was starting a new life in a new city and state, and a new exciting job.

Rebecca was exhausted from all that driving. Driving 1,500 miles in 3 days alone can wear anyone out. Rebecca marveled at her new condo, the kitchen was ultra-modern with stainless steel appliances like a Wolf Stove and a Sub-Zero refrigerator and a beautiful subway tile back splash. She grabbed a wine glass from the cabinet and poured herself a glass of chardonnay and headed towards her bedroom. She reached over and grabbed a sleeping pill that was prescribed for her and washed it down with the wine. Rebecca laid down on her bed and waited for the wine and pill to do their job. Rebecca only had a couple of days to rest before she started working for Thorton Associates and she wanted to be fresh. She knew that if she didn't rest she wouldn't be any good at her job. Finally her eyelids started to get heavy and she was asleep before she knew it.

The next day Rebecca began to wake up. Rubbing her eyes she forgot where she was for a moment. She got out of the bed and headed towards the window and opened the curtains. A violent thunder storm was happening outside. Rebecca had never seen so much lightning or heard so much thunder.

"Well there go all my plans for today. No going to the beach today." Rebecca stated out loud. Rebecca headed towards her kitchen and started to brew a cup of coffee. She sat at the breakfast bar and wondered what she could do today. "I hope that the rain stops. If I can't go to the beach, I could at least explore the neighborhood."

One thing about living in southern Florida, it rains almost every day for about an hour or two. Soon the sun would be out and Rebecca could drive around Fort Lauderdale. Rebecca finished her coffee and went to take a shower. She got dress, grabbed her purse and went to the garage. She drove down Las Olas and onto A1A and drove by the beach. The rain didn't keep anything wet for a long time since the sun was hot and dried up everything quickly. Rebecca put the roof down on her convertible and drove around the city. People seemed a lot nicer in Florida than they were in Massachusetts. She guessed being rude was just a Boston trait.

It was getting close to lunch time and Rebecca was starving. She pulled her car into a parking lot with a restaurant called J Marks. "This place looks nice." Rebecca entered the restaurant and was seated quickly. She decided to sit outside so she could enjoy the weather and the view. The menu was so diverse and everything looked so delicious that she wanted to order the whole menu.

"May I take your order?" Rebecca looked up and saw a very handsome young man. The waiter looked absolutely gorgeous, with dark brown hair and brown eyes to match. He had a slim build and a great smile. Rebecca was so jealous of his tan and his teeth were so white and perfect. Rebecca knew deep down that he wasn't for her, since he was obviously gay.

"My name is Jay, and I'll be serving you today."

"Hello Jay, it a pleasure meeting you" Rebecca replied with a smile. "Everything looks so good on the menu. Could you recommend something for me?"

"Well I love the blacken Mahi-mahi. It's a little spicy but so good."

"Well Jay, you sold me on the Mahi-mahi. I'll have that over a bed of rice pilaf and a house salad with creamy Italian dressing. Also, may I please have a vodka martini with Chambord and lime juice?"

Jay laughed "That's what we call a Raspberry Lime Ricky. I personally love those drinks. I'll be right back with your drink."

Jay hurried off to get her drink and put her order into the computer. Rebecca looked around and started to watch strangers inter-acting with each other. Watching people made Rebecca a better profiler. She could sit in a park all day and watch people walk by and figure out if they are married, gay, straight and what they probably did for work.

Jay came back with her Raspberry Lime Ricky Martini and placed it in front of her. "Enjoy!" Rebecca took a sip and sighed with pleasure. "Delicious." She said to Jay. "Give my compliments to the bartender." Jay smiled at her and nodded his head with agreement. "He'll be happy to hear a compliment." Jay left her table to wait on another table that was close to her. A handsome older gentleman was sitting alone. The man looked over and seen that she was steering at him. He smiled and lifted his drink to say 'cheers' to her. Rebecca lifted her drink and smiled at him while taking a sip of her drink. Rebecca knew he was about 30-ish and Latin descent. She could tell, even though he was sitting, that he was approximately 5 feet 10 inches. He was handsome but rugged at the same time. His hair was black and his eyes dark chocolate brown. He had a crocked smile and a cute dimple on his left cheek. Looking at him, Rebecca thought Puerto Rican descent and began profiling him. The voice in her head was chatting away. Rebecca could tell that he worked as a bar tender and was single due to the fact that he wasn't wearing a ring.

The handsome man arose from his chair and started to walk over to speak with Rebecca. "Hello, my name is Jorge Rosa and may I ask who you are?"

Rebecca smiled at him and told him her name. "Hi, I'm Rebecca Watson. Would you like to join me for lunch, or are you waiting for someone to join you?"

Jorge giggled a little at her statement. "No, I'm eating alone, so it would be my pleasure to join you Rebecca." Rebecca motioned her hand for him to sit with her at her table. Jorge raised his hand to signal Jay for another round of drinks. "So Rebecca, what brings you to Ft. Lauderdale?"

"I actually just arrived yesterday. I moved here from Boston." Rebecca said trying to profile him in her mind. "So what about you are you a resident or visitor?"

"I actually live here in the Wilton Manor's part of town. Where are you living? Did you find a good place?"

"Yes, I found a lovely furnished condo on Las Olas Blvd." Rebecca saw that Jay was coming to the table with the next round of drinks. "Boy these drinks are strong."

"I guess a little, but a lot weaker than how I make them."

"So you're a bartender I'm assuming?" Rebecca asked feeling kind of proud of her since she nailed his profession in her head.

"Yes, I am a bar tender at George's Alibi. It's a great restaurant and bar right in the middle of Wilton Manor's."

"I've never heard of it before, but then again I just moved here." She said laughing lightly.

"It's a gay bar with great music and entertainment. The drag queens that perform at George's are the best in town and of course the best bar tenders." He smiled at her as he took another sip of his drink.

"So, Jorge, what are you drinking?" Rebecca didn't want to ask if he was gay or bi but she knew she would find out soon enough.

"Oh, it's just a Shirley Temple. I don't drink Alcohol. I found myself indulging in too much alcohol when I was working at the bar." Jorge continued as he seen Rebecca most interested in his story. "I'm proud to say that I haven't touched a drop of alcohol in 4 years. I'm an alcoholic and it's easier for me to admit it now than it was 4 years ago. I realized that my drinking was interfering with my love life and work. All I ever wanted and thought about is where is my next drink coming from. I was drinking my life away." Jorge stopped to take another sip of his drink.

Rebecca couldn't believe that he was telling her all this after being just introduced. "I'm so sorry; I hope my drinking doesn't bother you."

"No, I work at a gay bar. I'm around booze all day." He paused just a little and started to ask Rebecca some questions. "So what do you do for work?"

Rebecca took a deep breath. She knew from experience, that telling people she worked for the F.B.I. drove guys away. "Well, tomorrow I start a new job with Thorton Associates."

"So you're a profiler?"

Rebecca looked shocked that Jorge knew what services the company provided. "Yes I am a profiler. I use to work for the F.B.I., but came here to work. I think working for a private firm is going to be better than a government job. How did you know what Thorton Associates did?"

Jorge leaned back into his chair. "Everyone in Florida knows what they do. It's a billion dollar enterprise. Also, I know the president of the company personally."

"You know Willard P. Thorton?" Rebecca asked with a surprise sound from her voice.

"Yes, I know Willard very well." Jorge continued with his statement. "He's a regular at George's Alibi."

Rebecca had to ask, even though she didn't want to know. "So is my new boss gay? Are you gay? To be honest with you I never met Willard."

Jorge started to laugh out loud. "Yes, I'm gay. I've been married to my great husband now for 5 years. His name is Miguel."

"Wow! That's awesome, but why aren't you wearing a wedding ring?"

"Well when Miguel and I were married, I weighed over 300 pounds. When I quit drinking and started to care about myself more, I lost the weight and the ring is just too big for me to wear, although, I do wear the ring on this gold chain around my neck. I have to omit that if I were Miguel I would have definitely left me, but he stood by me through thick and thin. No pun intended." Jorge smiled. "As for Mr. Thorton, he's neither gay nor straight. I would say he's more of whatever is available that night. He is an awesome guy, I like him, and he likes to tip. And he tips a lot! How the hell did you get the job without meeting the person hiring you?"

"Well since I lived in Boston all my interviews were via text. Mr. Thorton loved my resume' and offered me the job. He even bought the condo I'm living in and it's fully furnished. God knows I wouldn't be able to afford the place by myself."

"That's amazing! Willard is very generous with his money. I know you're going to love working for him." Jorge said encouragingly. "It's Saturday night and Willard, or Mr. Thorton to you, will be at George's tonight. Would you like to go with me? I'm working so all your drinks will be on the house. Plus I can introduce Willard to you!"

"That would be great!" Rebecca said with enthusiasm. "You know Jorge, I've only known you for 10 minutes but it seems like we're going to be great friends."

Rebecca didn't care one way or another if Jorge was gay. She was just happy to make a friend in a city she really didn't know. "Can straight people go?"

Jorge almost chocked on his drink. "Yes darling, straight people can go into a gay bar. Just don't go to Ram Rods. You would be shocked to see what happens there."

Finally Jay came over to the table with their meals. Rebecca's Mahi-mahi looked great. She looked over to see that Jorge ordered a Rib-eye steak that was perfectly cooked medium rare. The two began eating and chatted for the rest of the luncheon. "Jorge, here is my number, 779-555-5030, text me the address to George's. What's the best time to go?"

Jorge scratched his head as though he had to think about it. "Well happy hour is from 5pm to 8pm. I would say around 6pm. Willard usually arrives around 7."

"Awesome! I'm going to go home and shower. I'll wear something casual. I don't want to look like some whore off the street." Rebecca began to laugh at her own joke and Jorge followed suit.

After lunch the two of them parted ways. Rebecca was thrilled that she may finally meet Mr. Thorton. She was also happy that she met Jorge. Rebecca thought to herself that life in Ft. Lauderdale is going to be great!

CHAPTER 3

GEORGE'S ALIBI

Rebecca looked at her watch and seen that it was close to 6:30. "Shit!" She said out loud. "I'm going to be late." Rebecca phone alert went off and it was a text from Jorge.

'I had a great time with you this afternoon at the restaurant. I can't wait to see you here at the club. You'll be happy to know that there is a great drag queen performing tonight. I think you'll love her. She was on RuPaul's Drag Race. Her name is Plastique Tiara! She's absolutely stunning! I hope Willard shows up tonight, I really want to introduce you to him. See you soon my new bestie!'

Rebecca truly did make a friend this afternoon. A smile ran across her face as she was putting on her shoes. She was nervous about meeting Mr. Thorton. Was she supposed to know he was gay? Was she intruding on his privacy? These questions seem to torment her. She started thinking the worst case scenarios. 'What if he fires me? What if he meets me and he doesn't like me?' Rebecca started to panic. She took deep breaths and started to calm herself down. 'Remember Jorge said he's a real nice guy.' Rebecca started to feel better and finished dressing.

She jumped into her car and started to follow the directions that Jorge gave her to the club. When she arrived she noticed a lot of gay friendly establishments and a cluster of rainbow flags. She started to feel that Ft. Lauderdale accepted everyone no matter who or what you are, the feeling here was just pure love.

Rebecca parked her car and started to walk towards George's Alibi. The place looked busy. She remembered that Florida still had a happy hour whereas most states had abolished happy hours. As she walked into the bar she heard the music blasting. The lights on the dance floor area were flashing different colors to the beat of the music. Rebecca heard a voice from the distance calling her name. "Rebecca! Over here Rebecca!" Rebecca turned around to see her new friend Jorge working the back bars.

Rebecca couldn't help noticing that Jorge was hot. He was working shirtless and his chest and abs were perfect. Rebecca kept telling herself 'too bad he's gay and married'. "Hi Jorge, long time no see!" She said jokingly.

"Would you like to try my Raspberry Lime Ricky Martini?" Jorge asked.

"I would love to try it!" Rebecca yelled to be heard over the music. "This place is great Jorge!"

"It is awesome, and it's a great place to work." Jorge placed her drink on the bar and Rebecca lifted the glass to her lips. Jorge was right, he made her drink way better than the restaurant made for her that afternoon. "Oh my God Jorge, this drink is absolutely delicious!" Rebecca gave him two thumbs up for satisfaction.

"Thank you gorgeous." Jorge looked at his wristwatch it was getting close to 7pm. "Willard should be here at any time."

"I'm so nervous about meeting him." She took another sip of her Martini. "What if he doesn't want me to know he goes here?"

"You're just being silly. He won't mind seeing you. In fact, I bet you he'll be excited that he finally met the person he just hired." Jorge said as he walked over to another customer to take his order.

Rebecca watched in awe how Jorge made drinks. He was flipping the bottles, pouring drinks without looking without spilling a drop of alcohol. He definitely was a pro at bar tending.

Rebecca felt a tap on her shoulder thinking it was Mr. Thorton. She turned around only to see Jay from the restaurant. "Hey girl, what are you doing here?" He asked with excitement in his voice.

"Oh! Hi Jay, I'm waiting to meet someone tonight." Rebecca replied.

"Girl, if you're not a lesbian and you're looking for a guy, you're in the wrong place." Jay began to laugh.

"No, I'm waiting to meet my new boss. Jorge told me that he comes here all the time." Rebecca explained to Jay.

"Cool! What's his name?"

"Willard Thorton." Rebecca replied with a smile.

"No fucking way! Willard is your boss? That's awesome; he's such a great guy."

"That's what I keep hearing. Everyone, well you and Jorge, said he's great. I just hope I don't screw up or say anything weird that'll make him regret hiring me." Rebecca started to look around the club to see if she could spot him, even though she didn't even know what he looked like.

"I never caught your name? I'm Jay Robinson!"

Rebecca replied back "I'm Rebecca, it's a pleasure Jay."

"Well since Willard isn't here yet, would you like to dance?" Jay asked.

Rebecca shock her head yes and they both walked over to the dance floor. The music was loud but the beat was great. As they were dancing Willard walked into the bar without Jay or Rebecca noticing him. "That's your new employee on the dance floor with Jay." Jorge pointed towards the dance floor.

"Jay, do me a favor. Don't let Rebecca know I was here." Willard asked Jorge as he handed him a hundred dollar bill.

Jorge stuffed the money in his pocket and nodded his head that he wouldn't tell her that Willard was there at George's. "Your secrete is definitely safe with me Willard."

Willard turned around and left the bar in a hurry so that Rebecca and Jay wouldn't notice him leaving. Willard stepped outside and had an angry expression on his face. Willard didn't want any of his employees to know he was gay. Willard never had a boyfriend; he always paid young tricks for sex so that nobody would know. He didn't have time to settle down with anyone, especially a guy. Willard got into his Bentley and drove home. He knew that meeting Rebecca at George's just wasn't the right place to be introduced. "I'll see her Monday." Willard said out loud as he drove away.

After a few songs blared over the speakers over the dance floor, Rebecca was exhausted and Jay was sweating up a storm. "I have to take a break." Rebecca yelled in Jay's ear.

"Ok, let's get a drink!"

Both of them walked back to the bar and Rebecca noticed the time was close to 8 o'clock. "Guess he's a no show tonight." Rebecca said to Jorge.

"I guess so. I'm sorry!" Jorge replied. "Here's another Martini, on me." Jorge turned around and took a drink from the back of the bar and placed it in front of Rebecca.

"These are so good Jorge!"

Eight o'clock turned quickly to 1 am, and Rebecca was getting tired. "Sorry guys I have to leave. It's getting late and I need to do a lot of errands tomorrow."

Jay responded with a sad look on his face. "Are you alright to drive?"

"Yes I'm totally alright to drive. All that dancing you made me do had me sweat out all the alcohol I had in my system."

Jorge leaned over the bar and kissed Rebecca on the cheek. "Text me when you get home safely."

"Yes, text or call me also. I need to know if you're safe." Jay said handing Rebecca a match book with his name written inside.

Jorge handed Rebecca her purse that he kept safe behind the bar. "Thank you both for being so nice, I'll have you both over for dinner and drinks next week!" With that being said, Rebecca headed out the door and went to her car.

The drive home was quicker than she thought it would be. She entered her condo and texted both Jorge and Jay to let them know she made it safely home. Rebecca stripped naked and took a quick shower to rinse off all that sweat from dancing all night. She finally went to sleep around 2 am.

George's was closing and the lights came up in the bar. It was 3am and Jay didn't want to go home. He still had a lot of energy and decided to go to Jacobs Coffee shop to have a pastry and coffee. Jay started his car and drove off. He was driving down Route 1A and stopped at a traffic light. As he was waiting for the light to turn green, he felt the cold metal blade to his throat.

"Don't move, just keep on driving." The man in the back seat held a knife to his neck. There was nothing to do but to do as he said. Jay looked in his mirror to see a guy dressed all in black and a hoodie over his head. The sunglasses he was wearing were so dark you couldn't see his eyes. His voice sounded muffled and he noticed he had a surgical mask on. He couldn't make out any distinctive traits that he could use to identify who he was.

"If you want my money and wallet you can have it." Jay said with panic in his voice.

"Just shut the fuck up and keep driving!"

They drove around for hours that seemed like eternity for Jay. "Pull into that garage."

Jay did as he was instructed to do for he feared for his life. "Park the car right here." Jay pulled into an empty space. "Stop the car and turn off the engine, and get out slowly, and don't try to pull any shit or you'll be a dead man."

Jay once again did as the stranger asked of him to do. He turned off the engine and got out of the car. The man followed suit and stood behind Jay. Jay started to cry uncontrollably as the man told him to get on his knees. "Please just take my money and wallet and let me live." Jay begged the man not to hurt him.

The man mumbled something that Jay couldn't understand. He felt the cold blade of the knife penetrate his skin. The man slowly moved the knife from ear to ear slicing Jay's throat wide open. Jay held his hands to his neck and fell face first to the ground. The blood started to stream downwards heading towards the storm drain. The man then took his gloved hand and soaked it in the blood. In Jay's blood he wrote on the side of Jay's car 'sweet'. The man then walked away from the bloody scene and left Jay's lifeless body next to his car.

CHAPTER 4

FIRST DAY ON THE JOB!

Rebecca woke up Monday morning fresh and ready to start her day at her new job at Thorton Associates. She arrived 10 minutes early and was greeted by Sharon Dickerson, the human resource representative. "Welcome to Thorton Associates, I'm Sharon Dickerson and I will be showing you around this morning." Sharon was an older woman in her 50's. Her hair was gray and pulled back into a bun. She wore a white blouse and a black skirt with black flats. Rebecca thought to herself 'I bet she was beautiful when she was younger'.

"Over here is the café'" Sharon was pointing out all the main areas of the lobby. Sharon pressed the up button on to call for the elevator. "Your office is on the 17th floor." The door opened on the elevator and both of them stepped into the elevator. Sharon pressed the number 17 button and the doors closed and the elevator moved quickly up. It took only seconds to arrive at their destination. Sharon walked out and started down a long hallway until she reached an office. Rebecca looked and the office door already had her name on it. Sharon handed her the key to her new office. Sharon actually smiled at her and said "Welcome to Thorton Associates".

Sharon handed her a folder "This has all your operating codes and temporary passwords. Log into the computer and change all the necessary passwords". Rebecca sat in her high back brown leather chair. Her office was beautifully decorated with original art work. There was one painting on the wall that caught her eye. The painting looked like a Picasso. "This can't be an original Picasso?" Rebecca asked.

Sharon nodded her head yes "All the paintings are original dear, please make sure you lock your office door. We wouldn't want anyone to steal these beautiful pieces of work." Sharon smirked. Your direct line to your office phone is 754-555-2100. Your extension is 321; if anyone in the office calls they'll use that. A list of numbers is in your folder." Sharon continued to talk. "Mr. Thorton will be down at some point today. Also, here is your personal cell phone. The number isn't available to you so you can't give it to anyone. It's only used by Mr. Thorton himself. We all have cell phones that only Mr. Thorton will call you on. You must keep it charged all the time and do not shut it off." Sharon was about to continue when her cell phone rang. "Hello?" She just said a few words and the conversation was over. "That was Mr. Thorton. He has an assignment for you." Sharon was thrilled. She was only there for 30 minutes and she already had a job.

"That's great! What's the assignment?" Rebecca's voice was a little higher with anticipation. She couldn't wait to be on the job. She loved solving crimes that the cops couldn't do. She felted in powered by her knowledge in profiling.

"Don't get too excited yet Ms. Watson. Your assignment is to go to Ft Lauderdale High School and give a lecture on criminal profiling and answer questions from the students." Sharon was writing down the address. "Here is the address and you'll have to get going. The assembly starts in an hour and with the morning time traffic here you'll probably just make it."

"I'm not prepared to give a lecture? I have nothing written down, I can't go. Can someone else take my place?" Rebecca asked nervously.

"I'm sorry Ms. Watson, when Mr. Thorton gives an assignment he expects the person to carry it out. Saying no is almost like saying 'I quit'." Sharon continued talking to reassure Rebecca that she could do the assignment at hand. "You'll be fine Ms. Watson. I've seen your background and I've seen the percent rate of conviction from you. You're an amazing person. Just tell them off the top of your head. You needn't have any notes." Sharon thought to herself 'those high school kids are going to eat her up.'

"Thanks for the encouragement. I'll do it!" Rebecca took the piece of paper from Sharon. "Well I should get going. Thanks for the quick tour of the company Sharon. I really appreciate everything you have done."

"You're welcome dear! I think you'll fit right in here at Thorton Associates. We're all team players and it seems you are a team member."

Rebecca left the office and got into her car. She drove off and head towards Ft. Lauderdale High School to give a lecture to the students. She arrived on time and headed the too administration office to check in. Rebecca handed her credentials. "I'm here to give the students a lecture. Where is the auditorium?"

The clerk jotted down her name and credentials on a sign-in sheet. "The Auditorium is down the hall and take the first right and it's straight down the hall. Once you're there, just head to the stage and you'll be introduced by Principal Richards."

Rebecca thanked her and began her journey to the auditorium. She opened the door and saw the principle standing on the stage. The students hadn't arrived yet for the assembly. Rebecca climbed the small set of stairs to get on the stage. "Hi, Principal Richards I presume?"

Principal Richards extended his hand to greet her. "Good Morning Ms. Watson. Thank you so much for coming today. Mr. Thorton told me a lot about you. I'm sure the kids will love hearing what you do. Here at Ft. Laud. High we actually have a guest come in every week to speak to our junior and senior class for career choices. We found that so many children are lost when they graduate and can't figure out what to major in while they're attending college. We found that having these assembles the students are appreciative of the speakers. They tend to figure out what they want to be after high school."

Just as Rebecca was about to speak the school bell rang alerting the students the first period was done. "I'm happy to be her Principal Richards."

The students filed into the auditorium and took their seats. They were talking among themselves and chatted loudly. Rebecca reminisced about her time in high school and thought to herself that she was glad she was out. Principal Richards approached the microphone that was planted in the middle of the stage in front of an old podium and started to address the students. The second school bell rang to alert the students that the 2nd period was about to begin. "Good morning students. Please settle down and try to limit your speaking." Principal Richards waited until all the students sat in the auditorium seats and they actually stayed quiet. Rebecca was amazed how well behaved the students were. "Students it's my pleasure to introduce to you Ms. Watson. Ms. Watson works for an amazing firm called Thorton Associates." Principal Richards started to clap and the students followed suit.

Rebecca walked over to the microphone. "I would like to thank you Principal Richards for giving me that nice introduction." Rebecca faced the students and cleared her voice. "Good morning students of Fort Lauderdale High. As Principal Richards has said, my name is Rebecca Watson and I work for Thorton Associates. At Thorton Associates we work as an independent firm that helps police with major crimes. I am what they call a criminal profiler. It's my job to look at the evidence and crime scene to logically produce a profile of the criminal. In other words, we figure out who the suspect is and we arrest them." Rebecca could tell on the student's face that they were grasping every word that she said.

Rebecca went on for 30 minutes telling them about her time at Harvard University and that she graduated with a degree in psychology and criminal profiling. She also told them about her time at the F.B.I. and how many cases that was solved because of her figuring out who committed the crime. "So that's what I do for a living and I love it. Are there any questions you would like to ask me?"

Rebecca waited to if any of the students raised their hand. She noticed a boy in the second row who wanted to ask her some questions. "Yes, you in the second row, what would you like to ask me?" The boy stood up to ask a question.

"What's the first thing you look for at a crime scene?"

Rebecca only took a second to come up with an answer. "Well the first thing I look for is DNA. I look at the victim and the way they are disposed. If the victim is faced downwards, the killer has remorse and doesn't want to look at his victims face. If the victim is faced upwards, then the killer has a power ego. He needs to show his victim who is in charge." Rebecca noticed the young boy writing notes. "Are there any other questions?" Rebecca waited but no other students raised their hands. She thought to herself that her lecture was interesting enough for the students. If only she had enough time to prepare. "Well I would like to thank all of you and Principal Richards for letting me be here today." Rebecca turned around as the students in the assembly hall erupted with cheers and applause. Principal Richards shook Rebecca's hand and walked over to the podium.

"Thank you Ms. Watson. That lecture was very educational. Class you are dismissed."

The students started to walk out of the assembly hall and Rebecca noticed that some of the boys were shoving the student that asked a question during the lecture. She felt bad for him, but unfortunately, that's what high school kids do to each other. They bully each other to see who will become the alfa dog. Principal Richards walked up to Rebecca. "Ms. Watson, I thank you so much for coming in today. That was the biggest applause ever received by a person giving a lecture. You should be proud of yourself."

"Please Principal Richards, you may call me Rebecca." Rebecca said with a smile. "I thought I bombed out there since only one student asked a question."

"No, you were great. I could tell that the students were paying attention and retained everything you said."

Rebecca looked at her watch and noticed it was close to noon. "Oh my God, look at the time. I'm sorry Principal Richards, I have to leave and head back to the office. It was my pleasure coming here today, and please feel free to give me a call if you need me again." Rebecca handed him her business card and shook his hand and left the school.

Principal Richards went back to his office and turned on the microphone to the P.A. system. "Attention students. Corey Michael, report to my office immediately." After the announcement was made, he sat back into his chair and waited for him to arrive.

Corey heard the announcement while he was in algebra class. All of the students in his class started to laugh and chanted 'you're in trouble, you're in trouble'. Corey packed up his books and placed them into his backpack and started to walk to the principal's office. Corey thought to himself 'what the fuck did I do now?'

Corey was an intelligent student. Being only 16 he was already a senior and his GPA was a 4.0. Corey was a little rebellious with is dyed blond hair and his crop tops. Though he had beautiful golden brown eyes, he wore scary contact lenses that were either all black or with cat eyes. Corey only stood about 5'6" and weighed only 128 pounds and he always wore controversial clothing and never hid the fact that he was gay. He didn't have a lot of friends and his classmates usually teased for being different. Luckily he was never assaulted but being teased hurt him just as much as a fist would.

When Corey arrived at the principal's office the secretary told him to go right in to see Principal Richards. "Take a seat Corey." Corey did what he was told to do. He always respected his elders. "Do you know why I called you to my office?"

"No sir, I do not." Corey replied being as nice as possible.

"Well first of all I would like to thank you for asking Ms. Watson a question during the assembly."

Corey started to smile since he thought he was only called to the office for asking a question.

"How many times have I told you Mr. Michael that crop-tops aren't allowed?" Now Corey knew he was in trouble. Principal Richards' voice started to rise in anger. "Corey do you know how embarrassing it is when you stood up in the auditorium dressed like that and represent yourself as a member of Ft. Lauderdale High. Ms. Watson must be thinking to herself that the kids here are losers." He banged his fist on top of his desk and Corey jumped a mile. Corey has been warned many times about the dress code at school but didn't care about it. He thought that just because he was the smartest student and will be graduating valedictorian he could get away with shit like dressing the way he wanted too. "I've had it with you! I'm done with you Mr. Michael. Starting today you're on a 5 day suspension."

"You can't suspend me! That's discrimination!" Corey yelled back. "I'll call a lawyer!"

Principal Richards snapped back at him. "Go right ahead and call your lawyer." He turned around and took a booklet off the library shelf that stood behind him. He placed the booklet and pointed to the paragraph outlining the school's dress code. "It clearly states that 'no students, male or female, have an exposed torso or exposed nipples. So go right ahead Mr. Michael, call your lawyer. You're the one breaking the dress code. You're the one who didn't heed my warning time after time about wearing such clothing." His voice started to lower as he continued. "Corey, I like you as a person and you are a brilliant student, but you left me with no choice here but to suspend you. Think about it as a mini vacation and I'll explain to your parents that since you are valedictorian I gave you a week off. Also, it's not going to ruin your chances of going to Harvard since you've already been accepted and received a full scholarship. I hate doing this, but if I continue to look the other way Corey, all the other students will take advantage of me. You do understand why I'm suspending you?"

Corey shook his head. "Yes sir, I understand." Corey stood up from his chair and started to walk to his locker to place his books in it. He knew he wouldn't need them so why carry them home with him. Corey loved school and being out for a week was going to drive him crazy. Corey placed his books in his locker and closed the door and locked it. He headed down the hallway and walked out the front doors of the school giving it the middle finger as he left.

Corey started to walk home since he wasn't going to wait 4 hours for the school buses to pick him up. He lived approximately 5 miles from the school. "Five miles isn't going to kill me." Corey said out loud.

It was a hot and steamy humid day, and the sky was getting dark. Fort Lauderdale has some fierce thunder storms during the spring. Corey knew that he would need to take shelter soon before the storm hit. Corey heard the thunder that was crackling in the distance. "Fuck, any minute now it's going to pour out." Corey felt a few rain drops hit his head. Then a flash of lighting struck and the loudest crack of thunder shook the ground. Corey started to run for shelter but couldn't find anywhere to go. He knew standing under a tree was dangerous so he couldn't do that. Corey thought he was fucked when a car pulled over and the window rolled down and the driver spoke. "Get in the car; it's going to be a dangerous storm. I just heard on the radio that there are tornado warnings." Corey knew that getting in a car with a stranger could be dangerous.

"Sorry, but I don't get into cars with strangers." The rain started to come down hard and the driver of the vehicle showed Corey a badge. Corey looked at the badge and it read 'Broward County Sheriff's Department'. "Ok, thanks!"

Corey opened the car door and took a seat just as it started to rain buckets. "What's your name?"

"I'm Officer Jones, what's your name?" He asked.

"Corey Michael. Thanks for the ride. I've never seen it the rain come down this hard in my life."

"Well it is Florida; it'll stop within an hour." Officer Jones said laughing. "Why aren't you in school right now?"

"I was suspended for a week for wearing this crop-top shirt. I guess it's against the schools dress code." Corey explained to Officer Jones and started laughing.

"What's so funny?"

"Well, I guess I deserve to be suspended. I've been told a dozen times not to wear these types of shirts, but I wore them anyways."

"So you're quite the rebel l then?" He asked. "Well I have to say that I sort of agree with you. How can you express yourself if you can't be who you are and what you want to become. I can tell by the way you dress and walk that you have to be gay. Are you a homosexual?"

"Yeah, I am." Corey said to the stranger. "But I'm not embarrassed about being gay. My parents were cool with me coming out. Though some of the closeted cases at school tease me because I'm open and they're not. Shit, I've had sex with most of the boys on the football team. Yet they push me around like I'm a piece of shit."

"Wow! That must suck big time! Are you able to defend yourself?" The cop asked.

"It's cool. I know they're just doing it to protect their reputation. Plus they're not hurting me physically." Corey giggled a little. "In fact, they're the first to protect me from getting beat up. I guess they don't want me to have a fat lip and I couldn't be able to service them."

"That's one way at looking at things."

Corey noticed that the driver was very handsome. He really wasn't attractive to older men, but something about this guy he liked. "Have you ever fooled around with a guy?"

"No, it's not my thing. I've got a wife and 2 kids at home." He replied.

"I bet I'm better than your wife." Corey was trying to seduce him. "Come on, I know a secluded place near the everglades that nobody goes to. Let me thank you for saving my life."

Officer Jones thought about the offer and smiled at Corey. "Alright, but you have to promise me that you won't tell anyone about this."

Corey laughed. "I'm not the kind of person that kiss and tell. It's not my style. I'm very discreet."

The two of them drove until they arrived at the secluded area that Corey talked about. "Just park here, trust me, nobody comes here." Officer Jones turned the car off. "Now just relax." Corey started to go down on him just as he pulled a handkerchief out of his pocket soaked with chloroform. He placed the handkerchief over Corey's nose and he began to struggle. The more he struggled the faster he was becoming weaker. He struggled until his body went limp. Officer Jones opened his car door and dragged Corey's limp body out of the car. He dragged him about a hundred yards from the car. He stood over Corey and grabbed his hair to lift his head off the ground. He reached into his pocket and grabbed his hunting knife. "This should teach you not to get into a car with a stranger." He took his knife and sliced open his neck from ear to ear. The blood started to gush out of his neck as he held his head up to watch the red fountain of death.

The blood was now slowing down and he let go of Corey's hair and heard a thump as his head hit the ground. He put on a black leather glove and dunked his hand in the river of blood and just wrote the number "16" next to his victim. He then smiled at the gore he just made and dropped the fake credentials on top of his back.

He walked towards the car and doused it with gasoline and lite a match. He tossed the lit match into the window of the car and watched it be engulfed by the flames. He didn't want to leave any evidence whatsoever.

He walked out of the everglades and disappeared like a ghost. He left no evidence of him ever being there and he knew not to call a cab or Uber to pick him up so close to the crime scene. When he reached a good distance from the scene he called for and Uber. The driver arrived and picked him up. They drove off and the fake officer made an anonymous call to the police to let them know about where they could find Corey's dead body.

He had the driver drop him off away from where he really needed to be. He gave the driver a huge tip since he didn't speak any English. "Thanks for the lift." He closed the car door and walked away.

CHAPTER 5

THE AFTERMATH

"Car 19." A voice came over the police cruiser's radio. Detective Swanson picked up the receiver on the police scanner. He then responded to the call. "Car 19, over."

"Car 19 please head toward 125 East Sunrise Boulevard. Back up will be there."

"10-4 dispatch." Detective Frederick Swanson was a 25 year veteran on the Fort Lauderdale police department. He was a big burly guy who stood 6'2" tall and weighed about 260 pounds. He hated to shave and always had stubble. His hair was salt and pepper and his eyes were gray. His voice was low and raspy from smoking too much. Most people that knew him well just called him Fred. Fred wasn't an alcoholic, but liked his Captain Morgan and Coke after work. A little alcohol calmed his nerves from a tireless day.

He put on his police vehicle's emergency lights and siren. He swerved in and out of traffic until he arrived at his destination. A young man was standing outside of the garage. Detective Swanson showed the young man his badge. "He's on the second level. I found him dead." Fred nodded thank you and drove to the crime scene.

Detective Swanson drove his cruiser to the 2nd level just as back up arrived. He parked his car and walked over to see the victim lying in a pool of blood. The man that was outside of the garage was brought back to the scene by another officer. He was escorted to Detective Swanson. "Sir, this is the gentleman who found the victim."

"Thank you officer." Fred took a small note book out of his back pocket to write down information. "So, when did you find the victim?"

"I found him just a few minutes ago." The man said while holding back the tears from fear.

"Did you touch anything around the body? Like the car or the victim?"

"No sir I didn't touch a thing. I just called the 9-1-1 immediately after I found him."

"Very well then, the officer over there will take your name and statement from you." Swanson pointed to one of the uniformed officer who was taping off the crime scene.

Fred walked over to the body and saw the writing on the car door in blood. "Sweet?" he said to himself. He made sure that the person taking the photo's to capture the car door. The photographer looked at him and started to take the pictures. Fred looked down and saw the victim's wallet lying next to him. "Did you take a picture of this?" He asked the photographer. He nodded his head yes and Fred picked up the wallet and opened it. He noticed that there was money in his wallet and a lot of credit cards untouched. The license in the wallet read Jayson K. Robinson. With nothing being touched, this told him that it wasn't a robbery and it was probably someone he knew. "Check the entire area for evidence. And when the crime scene investigators arrive on the scene, make sure that they swab every inch of this car." Fred looked for any cameras around that would be helpful to him. He walked around the entire 2nd floor of the garage and headed to the ground level. To his surprise he noticed a camera at the entrance of the garage. He waved over a uniformed officer, and he promptly ran over to him. "I want any and all footage from that camera." The officer nodded and walked to the building that read 'security' only to find the door locked.

The officer yelled over to the detective. "Sir, the building is locked tight."

"Well find someone who can help you. Don't just stand there, be useful. There's a dead kid in the garage, and I'm sure he'll want us to capture the sick son of a bitch that killed him"

Fred walked around the garage and noticed a sign on another building that read *Monthly Parking ONLY $40! Call 754-555-PARK*. He took his cell phone out of his pocket and called the number. A sweet sounding old lady answered the call. "Hello?"

"Hello, this is Detective Swanson from the Ft. Lauderdale Police Department. Are you in charge of the garage located at 125 East Sunrise Boulevard?"

"Yes, I'm in charge. How may I help you detective?"

Fred knew she sounded like she was in her 90's so he wanted to tell her about the murder easily. "May I ask you your name ma'am?"

"Miss Sullivan. Kathy Sullivan." She responded. "Is there anything wrong officer?"

"Well Miss Sullivan, I'm calling you because there was a body found on the second level of your garage." He said it in a tone where he sounded sincere. "I was wondering if someone could come down and unlock the security office so that we may check the video tapes from the camera."

"Oh my, I'm sorry dear, but those cameras haven't worked since 2022." She said apologizing. "I tried to replace them but there so darn expensive."

"That's alright Miss Sullivan. Thank you for informing me about the cameras." Detective Swanson hung up the phone. "Shit! That was my only hope. Now I have to wait for forensics to find something."

Fred started to walk back to his car when a call came over his radio again. "Car 19 please respond."

"This is Car 19, go ahead dispatch."

"You're needed at 23 Old Mill Road."

"Ok, dispatch, I'm on my way." Fred was wondering why he was being pulled away from a murder scene. He got into his car and drove off to the next call. Old Mill Road was 30 minute drive. He knew it was no man's land. He was thinking he was going to find an alligator attack since the road hugged the everglades. Alligators were rampant there, and a lot of hunters go there to hunt. He figured one of the hunters got bitten or even killed by one.

Old Mill Road was a dirt road and on one side beautiful orange tree plantations and on the opposite side you have the everglades. There are no houses on the road but address numbers were giving as acre markers that lined the road. He knew that the number 23 was only 23 acres down the road. Up ahead he saw the emergency crew already had arrived. The fire department Chief was standing in the middle of the road while the EMS was sitting on the back of their ambulance. In the rear view mirror he noticed some police cruisers following him to the scene.

Swanson stopped his car right next to the fire chief and got out. He walked over to the chief and started to speak. "Hey Bill, what's going on? Why was I pulled away from a murder scene?"

Bill Dicker and Fred knew each other for over 20 years. Bill was a year from retirement and didn't want to retire but it was mandatory after 25 years. Bill was just as rugged as Fred was, with a bushy mustache and beard to match. His hair was as white as his chief helmet and he looked like a lumber jack. "Thanks for coming Frank. Sorry you were pulled away from your other murder scene, but what my men found I knew that you're the only detective that should be here."

"Bill thanks for the vote of confidence." Fred said shaking Bill's hand. "I haven't seen you in a few weeks. How the hell have you been?"

Bill looked down at the ground and started to change the social conversation to business. "We were called to the scene early this morning. The car over there was engulfed with flames when we arrived. After we extinguished the flames, one of my men noticed marks on ground like someone was dragged. He followed the track for about 100 yards and found a victim." Fred and Bill started to walk to where they found the victim. When they came across the crime scene tape that marked off the area Bill pointed to the victim. "He's young Fred. Only 16 according to his School I.D. badge." Bill was visibly upset about the crime scene. "His name is Corey Michael, 16 and goes to Fort Lauderdale High. That's all I have on the kid."

Fred put on some surgical gloves so he wouldn't taint any of the evidence. Bill handed Fred the I.D. badge and placed it into an evidence bag. Fred walked over to the body and found the lifeless kid lying there with his throat split open. He noticed a sheriff's police department badge and picked it up and he placed that in another evidence bag. He looked around and to his amazement he noticed the number written in blood '16'. Fred turned to Bill. "Hmmm, that's particular. My last crime scene the word 'sweet' was written in blood next to the victim on a car door."

"Do you think that murder and this murder are connected Fred?"

"I couldn't say right now, but they both had their throats cut open." Fred scratched his head and told the forensic team to take as many pictures and collect any evidence they might find. "I want you guys to pick through everything here. I want that car searched with a fine tooth comb. Just be careful, there are a lot of alligators in these everglades. I'm just shocked that the gators didn't eat the body." Fred walked away with Bill and arrived at his car. "Well I guess I'll be driving to Ft. Lauderdale High to learn about this boy named Corey. I'm sure the school will have his address on file so I can notify his parents."

Bill shook his hand. "I'm sorry Fred. I'm sort of glad that I don't have to do your job. It's tough enough when I have to report to a family member that their loved one perished in a fire."

Fred headed off to the school to talk with the principal. He hated to report that a child was killed. Fred found it disturbing that someone would leave the victim's age written in blood. And why was the word sweet written in the first victim's blood. Was it a sign of a serial killer? Could they have a deranged maniac on their hands? All these questions and more floated around Fred's head. He couldn't wait for forensics to come back with their findings.

Fred arrived at Fort Lauderdale High just as school was getting out. He walked into the school and made his way through a swarm of wild animals leaving the pen for dinner. He finally made his way to the administration office. An older lady was sitting behind the desk wearing horned rimmed glasses. "Excuse me; I'm here to speak with the principal."

"Do you have an appointment?" The woman asked.

"I don't think I need an appointment." Fred showed the woman his detective badge.

"Oh my, one second please. I'll see if Principal Richards is available." The woman picked up the phone and told the principal that Fred was here to see him. She hung up the phone and turned back to Fred. "You may go right in Detective." She pointed to his office.

Fred arrived at the door that read Principal Richards and knocked 3 times. Fred had a habit of knocking 3 times for some reason. He thought 1 or 2 knocks wasn't enough and 4 were too many. A voice from the office spoke. "Please come in."

Fred walked into Principal Richards' office and walked over to him. Principal Richards looked at Fred's badge. "Good afternoon Detective Swanson, what brings you here to Fort Lauderdale High?"

"Do you recognize this student?" Fred showed him the school I.D. badge found at the crime scene.

"Yes, I do know him. That's Corey Michael; he's our top student here and will be graduating valedictorian next month."

Fred felt terrible that he was about to tell him that Corey was murdered. "Would you have his contact information available?"

"Is there something wrong detective?" Principal Richards rolled his chair to his file cabinet and pulled out Corey's school record."

"Where was Corey yesterday?" Fred asked.

"He was in school for most of the day, until I had to suspend him for breaking the school's dress code." Principal Richards continued. "He left around noon yesterday. Please detective, please tell me what's going on!"

"Mr. Richards, I'm sorry to report that Corey was found dead this morning on Old Mills Road." Fred opened Corey's record and saw that both his parents worked at Pine Crest Auto. Fred knew exactly where that auto store was in town.

"Oh my God, not Corey. He was such a great kid." Principal Richards started to cry. "It's my fault entirely that he was killed. I shouldn't have suspended him."

"It's not your fault." Fred explained. "It looks like he might have been lured into the suspect's car by this badge I found." Fred showed the sheriff's badge to the principal. "Yesterday around noon we had a violent thunder storm. I bet whoever disguised himself as a sheriff, convinced him to get into the car and out of the rain."

"I still feel like it's my fault." Principal Richards picked up his phone and called his secretary. "Miss Rose, can you please come into my office?"

Miss Rose walked in Principal Richards' office. "Is there something I can do for you?"

"Yes Miss Rose, tomorrow morning before school starts we're going to have an assembly. Call Dr. White and Dr. Goldstein and have them attend."

"Why the grief counselors?" Miss Rose asked.

"One of our students has passed away."

"Oh dear, I'll get right on it." Miss Rose left the room and started to make the calls that Principal Richards asked her to make.

Fred stood up and shook his hand. "I'm so sorry for your loss Principal Richards. If there is anything I can do, please call me." Fred handed him his business card.

"Thank you Detective Swanson, I really appreciate it. If you find the son of a bitch that killed Corey, please let me know immediately."

Fred shook his head yes and walked out of his office with the names and numbers of Corey's parents.

Fred drove half way across town to Pine Crest Auto to talk with Corey's parents. Corey's parents owned and operated the business for 20 years. They only sold high end cars like Bentleys, Mercedes, BMWs and more. The Michael's were very rich and contributed to the community. Fred pulled into the parking lot of Pine Crest and saw how disgusting his car looked being parked next to a brand new Bentley. "If only I had two hundred grand to spend on a car." Fred walked into the show room and asked a sales person where he could find Mr. and Mrs. Michael. The salesperson read Fred's badge and pointed to the office at the top of the stairwell. Fred walked away and walked up to the office, knocked on the office door, and walked in. All the salesmen were busy with customers when a loud scream was heard coming from the office. 'No' was held longer than 'goal' by the announcer at a soccer game. Fred walked out of the office and Mr. and Mrs. Michael were holding each other tight. Their hearts were broken, and had every right to be angry and sad. No parent wants to hear that their baby, no matter how old they are, has died. Not to mention murdered. Fred mad a promise to the Michaels that he would find his killer.

Fred knew in his heart that if no evidence was found, it would be difficult in finding the person responsible for killing Corey and Jay, if both cases were connected. Fred also knew he would have to call in help if there are any more murders. Fred knew the best source to go to for help. Thorton Associates, the best criminal profilers around. Fred would only use them if he was stumped.

Fred drove back to the station and wrote up his reports on both cases. A folder was left on his desk. The name of the folder read Jayson K. Robinson. He opened the folder and read the contents and nothing stood out. The kid was clean although his alcohol level was pretty high. Fred shut the folder and scratched his head. "How do you kill someone without leaving any evidence whatsoever?" Fred turned towards the window and knew it was going to be a tough case to break unless the report from Corey would have something he could use.

CHAPTER 5

BAD NEWS TRAVELS FAST

Rebecca woke up to a slew of text messages from Jorge.

"Are you awake? Call me A.S.A.P.!"

"Hey, it's Jorge, call me!"

"I hate blowing up your phone, but it's important! Call me!"

"Jesus Christ Rebecca wake-up! Call me!"

Rebecca rubbed her eyes and read all the text messages from Jorge and dialed his number. "Good morning Jorge. Sorry about not responding earlier, but I always turn my phone off when I go to sleep. What's so important?"

Rebecca could hear in Jorge's voice that he was quite upset and was crying. "It's Jay, he's dead!"

Rebecca sat back down on her bed. "What? What do you mean he's dead?"

"They found his body in a garage with his throat sliced open. Rebecca who would do something like this to him? He was the sweetest guy I knew! It's not fair Rebecca, it's not fair!" Jorge started to cry uncontrollably.

"Oh my God, I'm so sorry Jorge." Rebecca tried to calm Jorge down. "Listen, I get off work today at 4, I'm going out with you tonight for some drinks and let's celebrate Jay's life together." Rebecca only knew Jay from the restaurant and at George's Alibi, but being a profiler she knew that Jay was a sweet kid.

"That sounds good Rebecca. I really need a friend to talk to tonight. Can we meet at J. Marks?"

"J. Marks sound good, and everything is on me. We'll meet at 4 after I leave work." Rebecca said goodbye to Jorge and showered and got dress for work.

Rebecca arrived at work on time and went directly to her office. She noticed a pile of files left on her desk with a yellow sticky that read 'review and file'. Rebecca sighed since she really didn't want to be used as a file clerk. She also knew that she was low man on the totem pole and shit work has to be done.

The day flew by as busy as Rebecca was, she liked being busy. She looked at her watch and noticed it was 4pm. "Shit, I have to leave or I'll be late." Rebecca got her things together and left work and headed towards J. Marks. Rebecca was so curious on who killed Jay and how his body was found. She really wishes she could see the pictures of the crime scene so she could examine them closely. Rebecca could tell a lot by just looking at photos. Though there's nothing like actually being at the crime scene. That's where everything tells a story.

Rebecca parked her car and headed for the outdoor patio where Jorge was waiting. She ran up to him and gave him the biggest hug. "I'm so sorry about Jay." Taking her hand she wiped away a tear from Jorge's face and sat across from him and held his hand. "Do you know anything?"

Jorge swallowed deeply and answered Rebecca's question. "All I know is he was murdered at the East Sunrise Blvd. garage. The cops are keeping everything hush hush."

Rebecca knew she had no clout with anyone at the police station yet, since she was only in town now for 4 days. She knew as time went on and people got to know her, then they'll give her professional courtesy. But for now, she's just here to comfort her only friend. "Although I just met Jay the other day, I feel like we could have been best friends."

"That's how everyone thought about him. He was loved by everyone!" Jorge took a huge gulp of his drink. "Why the fuck did I stop drinking!" He sort of giggled at what he just said. "Well Coke, do your thing!" He lifted his drink and made a toast. "Here's to Jay, a fun loving guy who will remain in our hearts."

Rebecca lifted her glass and they took a drink to celebrate Jay's life. "What was Jay like? Was he in a relationship?"

"No, Jay was single. He just got out of a toxic relationship. He wanted to whore around a bit." Jorge paused for a second. "Not sure how much you know about gay life style, but we can be pretty slutty at times."

"When did Jay break up with his boyfriend? What was his name?" Rebecca took out a note pad from her purse and a pen.

"Are you going to look into his death, Rebecca?"

"I'm going to try to build a profile. It helps me know a little bit about who Jay was and who might have murdered him."

Jorge sat up straight. "His asshole ex-boyfriend name is Dave Waters. He was way too old for Jay, and I kept telling him that. But he liked how Dave showered him with expensive gifts. Dave was in his late 40's and was so jealous at times. Jay couldn't even say hi to another boy without Dave giving him a dirty look." Jorge slammed his hand on the table scaring Rebecca. "If I find out that he had anything to do with this, I'll fucking kill him with my bare hands."

"Trust me Jorge; you don't want to kill him. I mean, I know you feel like you do, but let me handle this in a professional manner."

"I know you're right, but just thinking about it makes me so damn angry." Jorge finished his drink and ordered another round. "I only wish that I didn't have to work tonight."

Rebecca and Jorge talked for a few hours when he had to head to work at George's Alibi. The waiter came over and left the check, Rebecca noticed that the staff seemed undisturbed by Jay's death. She hoped to God that they just haven't found out about his murder. Rebecca picked up the check and Jorge tried to grab it from her. "No! I said I was paying." She placed 40 dollars on the table and they both started to leave the restaurant. "I'm going to do everything I can to find out who might have done this to Jay." Rebecca whispered into Jorge's ear while giving him a hug.

Jorge smiled at Rebecca. "Thank you Rebecca." He got into his car and drove to work. Rebecca started driving home and she made a call to her friend at the F.B.I. "Hey Luis, its Rebecca, I need a huge favor from you. Could you run a back ground check on a David Waters?" Luis agreed to run a check on David and Rebecca drove home to get some rest. The day was hectic and emotional, but she knew that just because she knew a person that got murder, she learned at an early age to put her emotions aside.

Jorge arrived at work and was visibly upset about Jay being killed. He turned around to Tommy the other bar tender and confessed his emotions. "Tommy, if I ever find out who did this, I swear I think I'll kill him."

The crowd started to file in, and Jorge became quite busy, too busy to think about Jay. Alibi's was busy no matter what day of the week it was, there was always something happening. Jorge was cleaning glasses and he heard a voice. "Who do you have to fuck to get a beer around here?" Jorge looked up and saw that it was Dave, Jay's ex-boyfriend. "What the fuck are you doing here? Your Ex just got killed and you're partying? Dave just gave him a smirk and asked for the beer again. Jorge took a deep breath and poured him a Bud Lite from the tap. "That'll be 4 dollars." Dave slammed a five on the table. "Keep the change!" Jorge took the five and placed the extra dollar in his tip jar. As Dave was walking away from the bar Jorge overheard Dave. "He thinks I should be sad that Jay's dead. The slut probably deserved being sliced up. I bet he was tricking himself out again!" Jorge had enough. He jumped over the bar and tackled Dave like a linebacker in a football game. Dave had fallen face first to the floor letting his drink go and smashing next to them. Jorge rolled Dave on his back and started to punch him as Dave covered his face. The other customers pulled Jorge off of Dave and calmed him down. Dave got up and was bleeding from his nose.

"You're going to pay for this you fucking faggot!" Dave shouted out while wiping the blood from his face.

"If you think you're fucking man enough, do it now! Come on sissy boy, come after me!"

There is one thing you should know about Jorge. He never backed down in a fight, nor did people talk bad about the people he cared for. Jorge was a true friend. He remembered one time, he and his friend Paul went out on Halloween. Paul had the best costume, it was rude and disgusting, but it was cool. Paul dressed as a priest being orally serviced by a boy. Everyone at the club cheered him on. The drag queen judging the costume contest wasn't impressed with his costume and she voted him off the stage only to let her drag-daughter win. Everyone started to chant 'Fixed! Fixed!' They all thought that Paul should have won fair and square.

Well, Jorge wasn't going to let his buddy down that night. He attacked the little bitchy drag queen that won and beat the shit out of him. Jorge was arrested that night, but charges were dropped against him since the drag queen never showed up for court.

Two guys held Jorge back so he couldn't do any more harm to Dave. Dave was escorted out of the bar by the owners who informed him that he wasn't allowed back in. "You're banned from ever coming here again!" Larry, one of the owners of George's told him.

Dave snapped back. "Fuck you and your fucking shitty club!" Dave left the premises and drove off.

Back in the bar Jorge was placing ice on his knuckles. Larry walked over to him. "Are you alright Jorge?"

Jorge shook his head yes. "I never liked that guy! He had it coming months ago when Jay showed up with a black eye. He said he hit his head on the kitchen cabinet but I knew that Dave hit him."

Larry patted him on the back. "Why don't you take the rest of the night off? In fact, take the rest of the week off. You need to mourn your friend. Your emotions are running high and I don't need my best bar tender in jail."

Jorge began to cry. "I really cared for Jay." Jorge was escorted to his car. He drove out of the parking lot and began his journey home.

Jorge drove east on Sunrise Blvd. He drove by the garage where Jay was found and a tear fell from his eye. Jorge noticed someone behind him was driving with their high beams on. The light was directly hitting his rearview mirror. "Fucking asshole, turn off your high beams!" Jorge slowed down to see if the driver would pass him. The car kept getting closer and closer to his car. "Jesus, why don't you just fucking drive on my ass?" He slowed down again and looked at his speedometer; he was now going 30 in a 40 mph zone. The car backed off and he started to accelerate again. He watched the car behind closely to make sure he wasn't going to do something stupid. The car behind him started to catch up to Jorge again, but this time he hit his bumper.

"What the fuck dude!" He started to go faster and the car behind start to accelerate again and hit his bumper harder. Jorge almost lost control of his car. The car behind him slowed down and Jorge started to race out of the area. He started weaving in and out of traffic. Fort Lauderdale was known for gangs that purposely hit cars. Once the driver pulled over to look at the damage, the driver would be mugged or killed by the gang members.

Jorge wanted to reach the nearest police station. He thought to himself that it could be Dave seeking revenge for beating the crap out of him. Jorge lost track on where he was driving and saw that he was on a road of a new development. He looked in his mirror and didn't see any cars behind him. He pulled over to the newly developed side walk and exited his car to see the damage to his vehicle. He walked around his car and squatted down to take a close look at his bumper. "Fuck man, I really don't need this shit right now!"

Jorge stood up and heard a screeching sound coming from behind him. The car that was following him was heading right towards him. The headlights were blinding him. He tried to move but his pants were caught on the broken bumper. He tugged and tugged, the car was speeding in on him. He had to get out of the way. He finally pulled his pants off the bumper and moved quickly. It wasn't quick enough. The driver smashed into Jorge's car pinning one leg between the two bumpers.

Jorge was screaming in agony. He looked down to see his femur sticking out. The headlights were shockingly still blinding him. He heard the car door open and the footsteps of a person walking towards him. Jorge was powerless. He couldn't run, he couldn't fight. He was at the mercy of this stranger coming towards him.

Jorge couldn't make out the person. He thought it was Dave. The drive took out a hunting knife from his pocket. Jorge could only see the glimmer of the blade coming towards him. The stranger struck his throat with the blade and Jorge grabbed his neck. The blood was gushing out squirting everywhere. Jorge was getting cold, he knew he was dying. All he managed to say before he collapsed on the stranger's car hood was 'forgive me father'.

After Jorge collapsed, the stranger took his gloved hand and dunked it in Jorge's blood and wrote the word 'killer' on the hood of his car. The stranger walked off into the woods that lined the street of the new development and disappeared.

CHAPTER 6

VICTIM NUMBER THREE

Detective Swanson arrived at the station the next morning at 8 am as usual. He poured himself a cup of coffee and walked over to his desk. The report about Corey was waiting for him on top of his desk. He sat down and took a sip of his coffee. He liked his coffee black but always had to add 1 or 2 sugars at work since the coffee was so bitter at the station. It definitely wasn't Dunkin's coffee. Fred opened Corey's file and saw nothing unusual, no drugs and no alcohol was reported. He looked over the medical examiner's report and did notice that he was contained by Chloroform. A tiny strain of hair was found under his finger nail and was sent out to a lab for further research. Fred hoped that DNA would be found and that whoever did this to Corey would be in the national data base.

Fred's phone rang. "Hello? Yes sir, I'll be there right away." He rose from his chair and headed off to the captain's office. Captain Ross Sullivan was a 30 year veteran. He rose through the ranks and became Captain quickly. Ross was a mean son of a bitch and didn't take shit from anyone. He was a short, bald, fat guy with an attitude of a Rottweiler. He was divorced 4 times and never had time for children. People always wondered what his ex-wives saw in him. Fred knocked on the door. "Come in!" Captain Ross said.

"Take a seat Detective Swanson." Captain Sullivan always kept it formal. He never used someone's first name, it was always officer, detective or whatever rank you were, that's how he addressed you. He was all about business, not making friends.

"Good morning Captain." No matter how much of an asshole the captain was, Fred always started the conversation with a cheerful greeting. "What's going on?"

"You have to go to a new housing development off of East Sunrise. A construction worker just called in and reported finding a person non-responsive. It could be a homicide or just an accidental death. Go check it out for me."

Fred stood up and began leaving the captain's office. "No problem Captain. I know exactly where they are building. I'll be there in 10 minutes."

Fred got into his car and started his journey to the new development. Accidents happen all the time at these sights and OSHA has a field day fining these companies. Fred saw in his rear view mirror an ambulance with their lights and sirens on speeding getting closer to Fred's car. He pulled over to let them by, since he wasn't in any rush to get to the scene. He noticed that the ambulance turned right down the newly developed road that leads to the housing complex being built. The dirt from the road was being pushed up by the speeding tires of the ambulance making it difficult to see the road ahead of him with all the dust being stirred into the air.

When the dust settled, Fred could see a pack of construction men standing around two cars and he noticed a man slumped over between the cars. "Fuck, I was called to a person being hit by a car!" Fred knew he had a lot of work to do with the 2 homicides that occurred in the past 2 days. He stopped his car and noticed the paramedics weren't attending to the guy between the cars. When he finally reached the scene he knew instantly that this was a murder. He noticed the writing on top of the hood of the car that read 'killer'. "Stand back everyone, this is now a crime scene."

Fred taped off the crime scene and called for backup and the forensic team. Soon about ten cruisers and the forensic unit showed up at the scene. "I want this whole place search for evidence!" The officers and forensic team hurried off and started to comb though ever bit of evidence they could find.

One officer ran over to Fred. "Sir, we're unable to get his wallet right now since he is still pinned between the cars. We don't want to move the vehicles until all the photos were taken. But we did find a registration that we believe belongs to the victim." The officer handed Fred the car registration. "The other car was reported stolen 4 days ago by a Mr. Thompson."

"Good job officer." Fred looked at the registration and ran the plate and information about the owner of the car. He was hoping that the victim and the owner were one of the same. "Car-19 over"

"Car-19 go ahead." The woman who worked in the dispatch unit replied back.

"I would like you to run this plate number and name for me." Fred continued his request. "Registration number 34 Charlie Delta Alfa 50, registered in the name of Jorge Rosa. Please run a search on the same name please." Fred put down his radio receiver and lit a cigarette. It only took a few minutes for dispatch to reply back.

The dispatch called Fred over the radio. "Car-19 over."

Fred stomped out his cigarette and picked up the receiver. "Go head dispatch."

"The registration on the vehicle is valid and is in good order. There are no outstanding warrants on Jorge Rosa. Over."

"Thank you." Fred now had to wait to see if this guy was carrying a wallet to check his identification. After about an hour that went by, the crew was ready to move the cars to release Jorge's trapped body. "Just make sure you're careful moving those cars." Fred instructed the first responders. As they began to move the car it was apparent that his leg was caught up against the bump. Fred looked down at where his leg was caught. "Poor bastard didn't have a chance." The coroner's office picked up the body and placed him into a black body bag. Before they zipped it up, Fred rolled him over to retrieve his wallet. He opened it up and sure enough it was Jorge Rosa. He wrote down his address and motioned the coroner to take him to the morgue.

Fred started his journey to the address that was on his license and registration. 33 Crystal Cove Way was in the Wilton Manor section of the city or also known as the gay section. When he arrived at Jorge's residence, he rang the doorbell. A tall Latino guy opened the door just in his boxer shorts. "Hi, can I help you?" Fred knew this must be his boyfriend or husband.

"Good afternoon, I'm Detective Swanson from the Fort Lauderdale police. Do you know a gentleman named Jorge Rosa?"

"Yes, he's my husband. Is he alright?" The man seemed shocked. No one likes a cop to be at your door. "Is he in jail? Larry from George's Alibi called me to tell me there was an altercation last night at the club. Did that son of a bitch David file assault charges on him?" Miguel Lopez was married to Jorge for 5 years. He was tall and thin and had wavy black hair and deep dark chocolate eyes. He was littered with tattoos from neck down. "Hi, I'm Miguel, Jorge's husband. Please come in." Fred walked into their house. It was like walking into a museum, art work on the walls looked original and the furniture was ultra-modern. "Please be seated, would you like a cup of coffee?"

"No thank you, Miguel." Fred wasn't sure how to let tell another person that their loved one is dead. "I'm here on official business Miguel. Tell me about David? Who is he?"

"Well to make a long story short, Jorge was very good friends with this guy Jayson, Jay Robinson." Fred interrupted Miguel.

"You knew Jay Robinson?" Fred asked.

"Yes, he was a good friend of ours until we found out he was killed. As I was saying, Jorge was at work and Jay's asshole ex-boyfriend arrived at the bar. I guess he started talking shit about Jay and Jorge went crazy shit on his ass." Miguel sat down on the couch and took a sip of his coffee. "Are you sure you don't want a cup of coffee? I just brewed it a few minutes ago."

Detective Swanson shook his head no. "So Jorge was working last night? What time did he get off of work? What's this David guy last name?" Fred took out a pen and his trusty notebook pad.

"Well, I'm not sure of the exact time, but he was sent home after the altercation. Larry called me about 10pm to ask me to call him when Jorge got home. When he never came home last night, I just assumed he was arrested. I guess I was right. I guess Dave Waters did have him arrested. How much will the bail be to get him out of jail?"

"Mr. Lopez, I've got some bad news. We found Mr. Rosa; he was killed last night at a new housing development." Miguel was noticeably shocked. He dropped his coffee mug to the floor. The mug shattered into what seemed to be a million pieces. Miguel started to shake uncontrollably. He was about to have a seizure right in front of Fred. Fred sprung to his feet and ran over to

Miguel and laid him down on the couch. He grabbed his cell phone from his pocket and called 9-1-1. The ambulance arrived within minutes of the call. The paramedics attended to Miguel and placed him on the stretcher to bring him to the hospital. "What hospital are you guys going to take him?"

"Angle Memorial Hospital." One of the paramedics answered"

"Ok guys, thanks for coming so quickly." Fred closed the door behind him and started to drive back to the station. He had 3 murder victims and at least 2 knew each other. He had to wait once again for the forensic report and the crime scene investigators to see if there were any connections to the victims. Right now he knew that each victim a word was spelled out in blood near the body. He also knew that Dave Waters was Jay's ex-boyfriend and he also had an altercation with Jorge.

When Fred returned to the station, he ran a back ground check on David Waters. A file came back with just minor infractions. "Let's see, unpaid parking tickets, and a misdemeanor for a domestic disturbance." Fred read the notes on the domestic disturbance.

Date: July 5, 2027

Officer King and Officer Hauser were called to 61 Wilton Drive for a complaint of a domestic argument. Both suspect, David Waters and Jayson Robinson were physically fighting with each other. After the two were separated, each was question to what had occurred. Jayson Robinson had noticeable abrasions that lead to the arrest of David Waters for assault and battery. Charges were later dropped by Jayson Robinson.

"Well it looks like I need to have a talk with David Waters." Fred closed the file and left the office and drove to the Waters' residence.

It only took Fred a few minutes to reach the residence of David Waters. He rang the doorbell and waited for him to answer. David opened the door. "May I help you?"

Fred showed him his credentials. "I'm Detective Swanson; may I come in and talk with you?"

David had cuts and bruises all over his face. His lip was swollen and he had the darkest black eye Fred has ever seen. "Please detective, come in, and make yourself at home."

Fred and David walked to the living room. David was wealthy but never flaunted his wealth. His home was decorated like a college dorm room. Instead of art work hanging on the walls, he had posters of gay icons like James Dean and Marilyn Monroe. "So how did you receive all those cuts and bruises?"

"Some asshole jumped me at the bar last night." David didn't know that he already knew about the fight in the bar. Miguel told him the whole story.

"Would that person be Jorge Rosa?" Knowing damn well it was him.

"Yes it was Jorge. Did Larry tell you what happened last night?" David handed Fred bottled water even though he never asked for one.

"No, I haven't talked to Larry yet, but I will. I'm here to ask you where you went after you left George's."

"After the bar I came directly home." He answered.

"Can anyone vouch for you?" David was wondering why the detective wanted him to have an alibi. After all it was just a bar fight. "Why do I need an alibi detective?"

"Well it's strange to me that your ex-boyfriend was found dead 2 days ago and you were fighting with Jorge that was found dead this morning." David remained silent after hearing Jorge was killed. "So do you understand why I want you to explain to me where you were for the last 2 nights?"

David started to worry and Fred could see it in his eyes. "I don't know what to say detective. I was home both nights alone. I swear that I had nothing to do with either one of their deaths."

Fred didn't seem to be convinced and had David stand up. "Well, I'm sorry, but you're under arrest for the murders of Jayson Robinson and Jorge Rosa." Fred had David turn around to cuff him and read him his Miranda Rights. Fred escorted David to the back of his car and the only words that came out of his mouth were 'I want a lawyer'. Fred hated when suspects lawyered up. He knew that he was unable to interrogate him any further once they asked for a lawyer to be present. Fred also knew that the lawyer he'll retain will be from a respected firm and not just a public defendant attorney. He also knew he'll need help with these cases. He had one suspect that was definitely tied to two victims but not with the third. He needs to call Thorton Associates to see if David fits this profile.

CHAPTER 7

REBECCA'S FIRST ASSIGNMENT

Rebecca woke up and went to work as usual. She tried texting Jorge but he didn't answer her text. Rebecca wasn't the type of person who badgered people. She knew he worked last night and was probably still sleeping.

When she arrived at her job, she noticed that her office door was opened. She found this strange since she knew she locked it last night and Sharon told her that she'll be the only one with a key to her office.

When Rebecca arrived at her office, she opened the door slowly. "Hello?" Rebecca said quietly. When the door was opened all the way she saw a strange man sitting behind her desk.

"Rebecca Watson I presume?" The man stood up and extended his hand. "I'm Mr. Willard Thorton." Rebecca was totally shock to see him standing there in her office.

"Mr. Thorton, it's such a pleasure to finally meet you." Rebecca was blushing like a little school girl meeting a teen idol for the first time.

"Nice to finally meet you too, Rebecca. Please be seated." Both Willard and Rebecca sat down at the same time. "You must be wondering what I'm doing in your office." Rebecca did wonder why he was in her office but didn't want to question him. After all, he was her boss. "I have an assignment for you."

Rebecca became excited. Finally an assignment, but she just hoped it wasn't another lecture for some high schoolers. "I'm overwhelmed with joy to have you on our team of criminal profilers."

"Thank you sir, I'm excited to be here also." Rebecca replied while blushing. Sher could never take a compliment too well. "So Mr. Thorton, what is this assignment you have for me?"

"Please Rebecca call me Willard. Detective Swanson from the Fort Lauderdale Police department needs your help. He has a suspect in custody but your profile will help him determine if the person he arrested is the killer of 3 people."

Rebecca perked up. Three victims equal a serial killer. "So he has a serial killer in custody and he wants my help?"

Willard stood up and was ready to leave to let Rebecca to get to work. "Yes, but he doesn't want you to see who he arrested until you see the photos of the crime scene to get your own perspective. Are you ready to take on the case?"

Rebecca replied with a simple node. "I'll do my best Willard to make you proud that you hired me." As Willard left her office she thought that he was a nice person and she was happy to finally meet him. She thought to herself 'so glad we met here and not at George's'. Rebecca knew that if she had met him there it would have been awkward. Meeting after work for drinks is one thing, but to bombard someone with your presents is another thing.

Rebecca picked up the folder that Willard left for her to take to the police station. A yellow post sticker was on front with the name of the detective she was going to meet. She placed the folder into her saddle bag and left the office to meet with Detective Swanson.

When Rebecca arrived at the station, the officer at the front desk called Detective Swanson to the lobby to escort her to the conference room he reserved. "Hi, you must be Rebecca. Mr. Thorton told me you're the best employee he has at his firm."

They shook hands and started to walk through the station. "So detective, I was briefed only a little on what you're working on. I heard you may have a serial killer on your hands."

Detective Swanson opened the door of the conference room that was quiet and very private. "I have someone in custody that has no alibi around the killing of at least 2 of the victims. He knew the first victim, Jayson Robinson."

Rebecca quickly interrupted the detective. "You're working on Jayson's murder?"

"Yes, I am, and 2 others along with him. Do you know Jayson?"

"Well, we met the other day at J. Marks and then that night at Alibi's. I was there with my new found friend Jorge."

Just as Rebecca interrupted him, he had to stop her. "You know Mr. Rosa?"

"Yes, I know him. I've been trying to text him all day but he hadn't answered me. I needed to know how he's doing after finding out his friend was killed."

Detective Swanson place the 3 files in front of Rebecca. She looked at the 3rd file and noticed the name 'Jorge Rosa'. "No, this has to be a mistake. Jorge can't be killed!"

"I'm sorry Ms. Watson, but he was found this morning crushed between two cars and his throat slashed opened. The poor boy didn't have a chance." Fred placed his hand on Rebecca's back to comfort her. "All three victims had their throats slashed opened."

Rebecca looked at all three victims and came across Corey's picture. "Wait, I know this boy." Rebecca made eye contact with Fred. "I did a lecture at Fort Lauderdale High the other day and he was the only one who asked me a question."

"So are you telling me that you're the common thread on all three cases?" Fred started to show her the other photos in the file. "Whoever the killer is he or she left behind a clue that I don't understand." He place the three photo's in front of her with the words 'killer', 'sweet', and the number '16'. "Two had words and the third had a number. I'm not sure if that's the number of people he killed or will be killing, or the age of the boy."

Rebecca re-arranged the photos on the table and spelled out 'sweet 16 killer'. "Is this the order you found the victims?"

Fred was shocked and impressed with Rebecca. "Yes, that's the exact order. Jayson had the word sweet, Corey with the number 16, and the last victim, Jorge had killer written next to him. Does this mean something to you?"

"It could mean something." Rebecca turned around to speak to Detective Swanson face to face. "Have you ever heard of a guy named Dr. Peter Monteiro?"

"No, I never heard of him. Why do you ask?"

Rebecca pointed to the three photos of the blood written message. "Dr. Monteiro was known as the 'Sweet sixteen killer' back in my home town Lynn. He was found not guilty on my 16th birthday. My grandfather was the detective that captured him. As he left the court room he threaten to take my life. It can't be him that committed these killings."

"Why is that Rebecca?" The detective asked.

"It can't be him because my grandfather killed him June of 2017. He killed 15 people in the mall that day. He almost killed me, but he ended up killing my grandfather. Both were shot in the head at the same time." Rebecca continued. "It was the worst day of my life. I still think a lot of people would have been saved if I just let him kill me." Rebecca started shaking and had to sit down.

Detective Swanson sat across from her. "So if this doctor guy is dead, who is imitating him?"

Rebecca knew that she was the target of these killings. "I think whoever is killing these people knows that I'm living and working down here. I think I'm the one he wants. The question is if Dr. Monteiro is dead, who is his copycat and why am I the mouse?"

"Well do you think you can build a profile on the person?"

"He's going to be a white male. Approximately 25 to 35 years old. He's probably single and keeps to himself. He will definitely know the history of Dr. Monteiro and my back ground. This guy is clever, and probably didn't leave any DNA evidence or finger prints at the scene. He knows his way around police procedures and also familiar with Fort Lauderdale. He's definitely a local guy that knows where the cameras are located and will not get filmed. He's particular in how he's killing these people by leaving his signature. Dr. Monteiro killed 34 kids and was found not guilty on all 34 charges. If this man is going to copy him, then more bodies will probably show up." Rebecca stood up. "May I speak to your suspect? If the person you have is truly the copycat killer, then he'll be nervous when he sees me."

Detective Swanson stood up. "That sounds like a brilliant idea." He walked over to the conference room door and opened it for Rebecca. "Follow me; the interrogation room is right this way. He's been sitting in there for 5 hours now."

Rebecca followed the detective to the interrogation room. She looked through the double sided glass mirror and seen David squirming in his seat. Rebecca walked into the room and sat across from him. David looked at her and Rebecca knew that he didn't know her or why she was in the interrogation room. "Mr. Waters, my name is Rebecca Watson, I'm sorry I kept you waiting this long." Rebecca opened her saddle bag and took out a pad of paper and a pen. "I've have a few questions to ask you. At any time during the questioning and you're not feeling comfortable in answering me without a lawyer, please let me know."

"I've got nothing to hide." David responded. "Ask me anything."

"First of all Mr. Waters, I am not an officer or detective. I work for an independent firm named Thorton Associates. I am a criminal profiler and I need to ask questions to figure out who killed your ex and Mr. Rosa."

"I know Willard Thorton very well, and I know what he does for work. He's a good friend of mine."

"Good, let's get started. You may answer the questions with just a 'yes' or 'no' answer or you're more than welcome to elaborate. Do you understand that at any time you may, and I repeat myself, ask for a lawyer?" David nodded his head yes and Rebecca started questioning him.

"Did you know Jorge Rosa?" Rebecca almost chocked up saying his name. She was devastated that she just found out her only friend in Florida was killed. But she also knew she had to be professional.

"Yes, I knew Jorge very well. He was a bar tender at George's Alibi."

"Did you and Mr. Rosa get into a confrontation? What was the fight about?"

David was getting agitated and Rebecca saw he was getting upset. "Yes, I fought Mr. Rosa. It was my fault; I shouldn't have made fun of the fact that Jay was killed. You have to understand, I was grieving. I loved Jay. I still love him."

"Did you know Mr. Michael?"

David gave a quick answer 'no'.

"Do you know how these 3 guys were murdered?" Rebecca opened up the file and took out the photos of all 3 victims and placed them in front of David. Within seconds, David started to vomit on the floor.

Rebecca interviewed David for an hour and packed her note pad back into her saddle bag. "Well thank you Mr. Waters, you've been very helpful." Rebecca stood up and shook David's hand and left the room. "Well Detective Swanson, Mr. Waters is definitely not our man."

"Thank you Ms. Watson, We'll continue to work with you. You've been very helpful." Detective Swanson waved a uniform officer over to him. "Will you please tell Mr. Waters he's free to go home? If he needs a ride home, please assist him."

The officer walked into the room and told David he was a free man. David walked out and passed Detective Swanson. "You better find out who killed these people."

"We'll find the son of a bitch Mr. Waters. And when we do, you'll be the first to be notified." Detective Swanson patted David on the back. "Thank you for all your help."

Rebecca watched as David left the police station. She turned around and spoke to Detective Swanson. "I'll send you my report by tomorrow with all the details of who you should be looking for that committed these murders. I'm at your disposal detective. Anything you need, just call and I'll be here immediately."

"Thank you so much Ms. Watson, I really appreciate any help you may provide. If you think of anyone that may be out for you, please call me. I'll drag them in for questioning."

Rebecca gave Detective Swanson a smile. "Thank you! I'm going to run my description to people that may know me and want to see me tortured."

Rebecca turned around and headed back to her office. She needed to solve this case before someone else gets killed.

When she arrived at her office, Rebecca started working on the case. Three people that she knew were murdered and she knew it was because who she was in the past. "Who the hell knows me in Florida?" She had to question herself out loud to clear her head. She called the office administrator. "Hi Sharon, this is Rebecca, could you please come to my office?" Within a few seconds, Sharon arrived. "Sharon I need a couple of favors from you." Rebecca looked up and saw that Sharon was just staring at her like she had 2 heads. "I'm going to need a white board in my office and I also need the help of another profiler. Do you have any suggestions who I should ask them to help me?"

Sharon responded like a snob. "Well, the only person I know that's better than Mr. Thorton would be Adam May."

"Thank you Sharon." Sharon turned around and left Rebecca's office just as fast as she came. Rebecca left her office to find Adam's office. His office was only a few doors down from her which would make it easier to work together. Even though Rebecca was the best in the business, she needs help because of Dr. Monteiro. She knocked on the door and a young sounding voice answered. "Come on in, the doors unlocked." Rebecca entered his office, and just like her office it was decorated with priceless artwork that should be hanging in a museum. "Hi Adam, I'm Rebecca Watson, I just started here a couple of days ago. I was wondering if you could assist me on a case that was just handed to me."

Adam stood up and introduced himself formally. "Hi Rebecca, it's a pleasure meeting you. How may I assist you?" Adam looked like a Greek God. Blond spiked hair, brown eyes, and a muscular physique. Rebecca estimated his age at 30, and when he stood up he stood 6 feet tall.

Rebecca loved how everyone in the office was a team player. "Well Adam, I just left the Fort Lauderdale police department and spoke with Detective Swanson. He has a killer on his hands that has already killed 3 people."

Adam sat back down behind his desk and motioned Rebecca to have a seat. "I thought I was told you were the best in the business." He said with a little smirk on his face.

Rebecca knew he was just teasing her so she had to tease him back. "I am the best." They both started to laugh. "Seriously though, I have to have someone else look at these files since I think that I'm the connecting thread that bonds these three victims."

Adam scratched his head. "I have to ask, why do you think that?"

Rebecca told him the whole story about the sweet sixteen killer and how he met his death by her grandfather. She also told him how he threatened her life back in 2017.

"Well if Dr. Monteiro is dead, who would be leaving you these clues?"

"That's the problem with this case. I don't know anyone here in Ft. Lauderdale, and I just met Jayson, Jorge, and Corey I met in school during my lecture."

Adam read the files and looked at the photos of the 3 victims. "Well my professional guess would be he's a white male, approximately your age. He doesn't know these victims since I don't see any remorse in these photos. I really think it could be someone in your past. We can start there tomorrow."

Rebecca stood up from her chair. "I really appreciate all your help."

Adam smiled at her and Rebecca started to blush a little. She found him really attractive and would love to ask him on a date, but she never dates anyone that she worked with. "Why don't we meet together tonight for dinner and discuss the case. I know a really good Italian restaurant named Bistro Mezzaluna. The food there is fabulous and they make the best Cosmo martinis."

Rebecca thought it over for a few seconds and came to the rational that it's just a business dinner. "That sounds great."

"Perfect, we'll meet at 7. My treat and I won't take no for an answer."

"Fine, but the next dinner is on me." Rebecca smile at him and started to leave his office.

"Rebecca, before you leave, just bring any personal telephone books you may have with the numbers of the people in your past. We'll write down all the suspects that fit our profile and call them to find out what they have been up too."

"That's a great idea! I'll bring my year book too and we can go through that to see how many guys fit the description." Rebecca left and went home to prepare.

Once she arrived at her condo she opened her door and notice a sealed letter was slid under her door. Rebecca opened the letter and all it said was 'guess who'. Rebecca scrambles around her condo and went to the secured lobby and saw the valet standing guard. "Hi, have you been working all day?"

"Yes I have ma'am. How may I help you?" The valet guy stood there in his newly pressed uniform and kept vigil for any visitors.

"Do you have a log of visitors coming and going?"

"Yes ma'am, I do. Would you like to see it?"

"Yes and any video footage you may have?"

"Sorry ma'am, I'm not able to show you that since the camera's in this building all died yesterday. The management company is having someone to fix them tomorrow."

The man handed Rebecca the visitors log book. She scanned the pages and only 2 men signed into the log. Rebecca wrote down the 2 names and went back to her apartment. She grabbed her phone and texted Adam.

Adam, its Rebecca, someone slipped a note under my apartment door. Written in blood were the words 'guess who'? I looked at the visitors log book and wrote down the only two male names listed. We should definitely check these two guys out. Unfortunately the buildings security cameras are not working, so there aren't any photos of these two men. I'll see you at 7.

Rebecca took a quick shower and got dress for dinner with Adam. She looked down at her work phone and Adam still hadn't texted her back. Rebecca shrugged it off since she was meeting him in 30 minutes at the Bistro. She placed the blood written note into her bag and left her apartment. When she arrived at the restaurant she was 15 minutes early so she decided to grab a drink at the bar. She took a stool where she could see people coming and going so if Adam showed up she would greet him. Rebecca ordered her usual Raspberry Lime Ricky Martini and took a sip of it and gave thumbs up to the bartender. All she could do now is sit and wait for Adam to arrive.

CHAPTER 8

DISASTER!

The following day Rebecca went to work furious. Adam had stood her up for dinner. She knew it wasn't a date, but work needed to get done and she wasted 2 hours of her time waiting for him to arrive.

Rebecca stormed into Adam's office. "Where the hell were you last night? I waited for you for 2 hours. I ended up having dinner by myself."

Adam looked up. He was visibly upset about something. "Did you get a text from Mr. Thorton?"

"No, I sent you a text last night and never got a reply from you either. What did Mr. Thorton want?"

"Rebecca, you better sit down." Adam instructed. "Sharon was killed last night." Rebecca was caught off guard with this terrible news. "She was found at the Bonnet House Museum and Gardens with her throat slashed open." Adam handed Rebecca his phone with Mr. Thorton text about Sharon.

It gives me great grief to inform you that our beloved administrator, Miss Sharon Dickerson, was murdered last night. Detective Swanson from the Fort Lauderdale Police Department has informed that he was called to a scene at the Bonnet House Museum and Garden. He said that her body was found in the middle of the garden by hikers early last night around 6pm. An investigation has been opened. We at Thorton Associates extend our sincere sympathy to her family. Sharon was a part of our family and when the funeral arrangements are made I am instructing all of us to attend. There will be no work that day. Let's keep Sharon's family and friends in our prayers.

Rebecca trembled handing the phone back to Adam. "Do you think she's connected to the others who were killed the same way?"

Adam just shook his head. "I haven't been able to see any of the crime photos or police reports yet."

Sharon took out her phone and it started to ring. "This can't be good news its Detective Swanson calling." She answered her phone to speak with the detective. "Detective Swanson, I just heard about my co-worker Sharon."

"Miss Watson, I extend my deepest sympathy to you and all of the associates at Thorton. I need you to come to the station."

"I'm on my way detective. I'll be there in 30 minutes." Rebecca hung up the phone. "I think she's a part of the sweet sixteen murders." Rebecca's voice cracked a little. "Adam, everyone coming in contact with me is being killed. Who the fuck is killing all these people?"

Adam stood up and gave Rebecca a hug. "Would you like me to come with you to the police department?" Rebecca looked into Adam's eyes and nodded yes to him. "Ok, I'll get my things together. We'll take my car. I want to know who the fuck did this to Sharon."

Both Adam and Rebecca drove to the Fort Lauderdale police station. Rebecca took out the note that was left in her Apartment. "What's that?" Adam asked.

"This note was slipped under my door of my apartment last night. I text you about it last night on your business phone."

Adam looked at the note. "Guess who? Is that written in blood?"

"I think it is blood. I'm going to have Detective Swanson run a DNA test. It could be the victims or it could be the killer's blood. I'm hoping that it is his DNA so at least we could have a definite lead."

They pulled up to the police station and were automatically escorted to the conference room where Rebecca and the detective were before. They walked into the room and noticed that there was a board set up with the victims pictures posted on it. It also showed the bloody wording that the killer left behind as a clue. Rebecca knew instantly that Sharon's death was a part of the investigation since she seen her picture posted. Underneath the picture the words 'guess who' was left behind in blood.

"Thank you for coming so quickly." The detective walked in the room and startled both Rebecca and Adam. "And who might you be?"

Adam extended his hand. "I'm Adam May, I work with Rebecca."

"Thanks for coming down Adam; I'm sure we'll need another set of eyes to figure out who is doing all the killings."

"I see that Sharon is among the victims." Rebecca pointed to the board.

"Unfortunately she was a victim, that's why I called you in. She makes the 4th victim with ties to you Rebecca. I'm beginning to wonder if you're going to be a suspect or victim." He sat down at the conference table. "Where were you last night between the hours of 6pm and 8pm?"

"You think I'm the killer? Are you fucking with me?" Rebecca crossed her arms and you could tell she was angry. "Not that it's your business since I'm not the one doing this, but I was at Bistro Mezzaluna from 6 till 9. I'm sure the restaurant has footage of me being there and they'll be able to vouch for me."

"I'm sorry Rebecca, but I had to ask." The detective really seemed to be apologetic and Rebecca new deep down he was just doing his job. "Now that I know you're not a suspect, we definitely know the killer is sending you messages."

Rebecca pulled out the note from her purse. "This was slipped under my door last night before I arrived home from work. There were on two male visitors on the log at the condo. Unfortunately the cameras are all disabled at the moment." She took the letter out of the envelope and unfolded it to reveal the message written in blood. "I was hoping that your crime scene investigators could run a DNA test on the blood. My finger prints are all over it so I'm sure they'll get a hit off the national data base since I was an FBI agent. I'm hoping that there is another set of prints though."

Rebecca handed the note to Detective Swanson as he placed rubber gloves on his hand so he wouldn't contaminate the evidence. "I'll put it in the evidence bag and have them run prints and DNA." Detective Swanson called in a uniformed officer to take the evidence bag down to the crime lab. "Tell the lab I need this A.S.A.P." He ordered the officer to make it quick. "Don't just stand there like a fucking lump on a log, go!"

The officer hurried off with the evidence. "We'll have the results in an hour or so, would you like to wait around?"

Both Rebecca and Adam replied simultaneously "Sure, we'll wait!"

As all three were looking for any clues in the photos, no one noticed that 3 hours had gone by. Detective Swanson looked at his watch. "What the fuck is taking them so long." The detective picked up the conference room phone and dialed the number to the lab. "This is Detective Swanson, I sent an envelope to the lab and I want to know what the prognosis." Detective Swanson said a lot of yes' during the conversation. "Thank you, and next time don't forget to call me." The detective hung up the phone and looked at Rebecca. "What's the name of the guy who was killed in 2017?"

Rebecca looked up from the pile of photos she was examining. "Dr. Peter Monteiro. Why do you ask?"

"Well the reason why the test took so long to complete is because the person used the blood of someone who is supposed to be dead."

"What? Are you telling me that Dr. Peter Monteiro could be alive? I watched him fall on the mall floor after my grandfather shot him in the head. Seen his brains splatter on the window of Macy's."

Adam chimed in the conversation. "I have a theory. What if the killer knew the doctor and was able to get a vial of his blood and froze it?"

"But why are they doing this to me now? It's been ten years." Rebecca couldn't understand what was really happening to her.

"We'll figure this out Rebecca." Adam said while hugging her again. "I'm going to help you until we find this son of a bitch." Adam kissed her softly on her cheek. "Do you still have the names of the people that visited your condo complex?"

"Yes, it's right here." Rebecca pulled out the paper with the two names on it with their phone numbers and addresses. "Both were luckily listed in the phone book."

Detective Swanson took the paper from Rebecca's hand. "Well I say that I'm going to make a visit to Mr. Hamilton and Mr. Chase."

"Can we tag along with you detective?" Adam asked. "We would love to come with you."

"Follow me." Detective Swanson commanded like a true leader. All three of them walked through the station and stood in front of a woman working like crazy. "Excuse me Linda. Could you do me a favor?"

"You want me to grant you another favor Fred? How many does that make this week?" Linda Staples looked at the detective like she was joking with him.

The detective handed her the paper with the names and address of the two guys that had visited Rebecca's condo complex. "Can you run these names through the computer and see if anything comes up?"

Linda typed in the name of the first suspect Jamie Hamilton. "The computer is coming up blank on this guy." Linda typed in the name of the second suspect January Chase. "Now this is interesting."

"What's so interesting Linda?" Adam asked.

"Well, it seems that Mr. Chase has an outstanding warrant for not showing up for his court hearing. He was charged with criminal assault with a dangerous weapon. A hunter's knife was used in the altercation. He slashed the defendant's throat just barely missing the jugular vein." Linda turned around and gave Detective Swanson a print out of the rap sheet the suspect had accumulated. "Here is his last known address and phone number. I highly doubt that the phone number is working and if I was on the run, I wouldn't be at the last known address either."

"Thanks Linda, you're a peach." Detective Swanson took the print out from Linda. "So let's give Mr. Jamie Hamilton a visit first. The three of them set off in their own cars and followed the detective to the first suspect's home at 37 SE 19th Street. Just south of Las Olas Boulevard where Rebecca lived.

When the three of them arrived at Mr. Hamilton's home, Detective Swanson rang the doorbell. They waited for 5 minutes before they heard someone about to answer the door. The door opened and there stood an elderly man hunched over holding his cane. With a very shaky voice the guy spoke. "May I help you?" Looking at him they knew instantly that this man couldn't be the killer.

Detective Swanson introduced himself and us to Mr. Hamilton. "Are you Mr. Jamie Hamilton?" The guy must have been in his 80's. He was bald with patches of age spots all over his scalp, face and neck. His skin on the neck was loose as a turkey's wattle. His hands trembled probably from Parkinson's disease. He had trouble focusing his eyes to see who was at the door. His eyes were once green or hazel but have now diminished from the cloudiness that the cataracts cause. "Hi, I'm Detective Swanson and this is Ms. Watson and Mr. Adams from Thorton Associates. Were you at the Sun Rising Condo complex on Las Olas yesterday?"

"Why yes I was detective, I was visiting my friend Harvey Goldstein." Mr. Hamilton was confused why the police were at his door. "Did I do something wrong officer?"

Detective Swanson placed his hand on the elderly man's shoulder. "No you did nothing wrong Mr. Hamilton, we're here to see who visited the condo since there is no video of who checked in the building." The detective tried to explain without giving him the real reason why we were at his home. "They found a lost kitten so we're trying to find its owner." Rebecca was trying to hold in her giggles with the excuse that the detective gave to Mr. Hamilton.

"Well I assure you officer it's not my cat. I'm highly allergic to them." His squeaky voice was almost comical like Mr. Magoo.

"Thank you Mr. Hamilton, I'm sorry to have disturbed you."

"No trouble at all officers. I hope you find the owner of the cat." Mr. Hamilton slowly closed the door behind him.

"Well it's definitely not him." Rebecca said.

Adam agreed with her with a laugh. "I agree with Rebecca. He doesn't fit out profile of a white male between the ages of 27 to 35. Plus, I don't think Mr. Hamilton could kill a fly."

"Well I guess we're off to the other side of town. Mr. Chase lives off of North Federal Highway, NE 26th St. I doubt he'll be there, but it's worth a try." Detective Swanson started to walk to his car. "I'll meet you two there." He entered his car and drove off. Rebecca and Adam slowly walked to their car.

"Do you think he'll be there?" Rebecca asked Adam.

"I highly doubt it since he is a fugitive. I know if I was on the run, the last place I'd be is my house." Rebecca knew that what Adam just said was true. You'd have to be an idiot to be at your last known address. The two of them got into their car and drove to the address that Detective Swanson gave them. Rebecca was happy that Adam was driving. She was still new to the city and wouldn't know how to find the address of the next suspect. Adam seemed to know exactly where he was going. He took the scenic route driving by the beach. It was a beautiful day and the beach was packed with Floridians and tourists. She wished she were a part of the fun activities the people were having at the beach. Adam's car came to a sudden stop. "I hate these fucking draw bridges. They take forever to go down." Adam put his car in neutral and started to talk with Rebecca. "So Rebecca, are you enjoying Fort Lauderdale?" Adam realized what he just asked her. "Oh, my God. I'm so sorry Rebecca. You must think I'm an idiot for asking you the most stupid question on earth. Especially what's been going on since you arrived here in Florida. Can you ever forgive me?"

"Don't be silly Adam. I know you were just trying to make small talk with me. I'm not insulted and you shouldn't be ashamed of yourself for asking." Rebecca grabbed hold of Adam's hand. "To tell you the truth, besides everyone I know ending up dead, I really like it here in Fort Lauderdale. The weather is fantastic. The people are ultra-friendly. And most of all, I love my new job and you're the best co-worker a girl could have."

Adam squeezed Rebecca's hand and smiled at her as the he started to shift his car into drive. The draw bridge finally closed and they drove onto North Federal Highway. "Hey, that's J Marks. That's the first restaurant I ate at and where I met Jorge and Jay. I had no idea what this street was named, but now I do."

Adam took a right on the NE 26th ST. and saw the detective waiting for them to arrive. "What took you two so long?"

"One word detective, drawbridge!" Adam answered.

"They are everywhere down this part of the state." Detective Swanson turned around and stopped Rebecca and Adam. "Wait right here, he may be dangerous." Detective Swanson walked to the door and banged on it. "Open up, Police!" He looked through the pain of glass and didn't see anything moving around. "Do you guys hear that scream?" Both Adam and Rebecca turned to each other and looked confused until they saw the detective kick down the door. Adam and Rebecca knew he needed a search warrant to enter the house, but if he had plausible cause, he could enter without a search warrant.

Adam and Rebecca waited outside until the detective gave them the okay to enter. Neither of them carried a gun so they were helpless if Chase was there with a firearm. "Place is clear." Detective Swanson motioned them to enter the home. As they both walked in, they gathered profiling information just on the condition of the home. "So, what do you two think?"

Rebecca looked around the house. It was a pig sty, filth everywhere you looked. "He's definitely not organized so I really doubt he killed those people. All the crime scene photos showed that the killer was particular on how he left the scene leaving no evidence behind. This guy is incapable of being that organized."

Adam gave his own opinion. "I agree with Rebecca, this guy is not the killer. We're looking for someone who is very well organized and hates messes. This guy lives in filth which tells me he's not who we're looking for. Although, he could be the guy who slipped the note under Rebecca's door. We should still question him to see if he was paid to leave that note."

"I have an idea. Why don't we go to his mother's house and have her call her son over. When he gets there we can interrogate him." Rebecca said.

"That plans sounds good to me." Adam replied. "How about you detective, are you interested?"

"That's a brilliant idea, Rebecca. We should get going." Detective Swanson said as he was walking towards the door. He turned around and saw that Rebecca was picking up a hair brush off the coffee table. "What's that for?"

"I'm taking this to the lab for DNA samples. You'll never know what you'll find out about this guy." Rebecca took the brush and placed it into an evidence bag. All three drove to Rebecca's condo. Once all three arrived at Sun Rising Condo complex, Rebecca opened the main door. They all entered the elevator to the 7th floor where January's mother resided. Rebecca knocked on the door and a woman's voice could be heard from the other side.

"I'm coming, I'm coming." The woman's name was Sylvia Chase. She's a widow and mother of 3 children, Chase being the oldest. Sylvia opened the door and seen the three of them standing there. "May I help you?"

Detective Swanson flashed his badge. "Good afternoon Ms. Chase, I'm Detective Swanson, this is Rebecca Watson, and Adam May. May we come in and talk to you about your son Chase?"

Sylvia waved them into her condo. The place was neat and organized unlike her son's house. The furniture was traditional style and was well taken care of. "Come on in, would you like something to drink?" Rebecca thought how polite people were in Ft. Lauderdale, unlike the people in D.C. or Virginia. "Please, have a seat."

"Thank you Ms. Chase." Detective Swanson began his questioning. "Would you know where your son is or how to get a hold of him?"

"I haven't seen him in weeks." Sylvia lied about seeing her son the other day, since she thought she was protecting him.

"Ms. Chase, may I call you Sylvia?" Adam asked politely.

"Sure honey, you may call me anything you want." Sylvia was noticeably attractive to Adam and started flirting with him. "I love police men."

Feeling a little uncomfortable, Adam continued. "Thanks Sylvia, but I'm not a cop. Rebecca and I work for Thorton Associates. We know your son was here just the other day. He logged in with the concierge at the front desk."

"Oh, that's right, it was just the other day I saw him. Old age honey, we forget things." Sylvia started to laugh a little. "Why are you guys looking for him?"

Detective Swanson stood up and stretched. He walked over to the sliding glass doors to admire the view from her condo. He was able to see the Intracoastal Waterway. "Lovely view you have Sylvia. Your son Chase has an outstanding warrant for his arrest for not showing up for court on charges of assault with a deadly weapon. Now, we know he was here visiting you. What I want you to do is tell us why he was here and why you were harboring a known fugitive?"

"He was here for a visit. He said he had to come here and deliver something to somebody who lived here. I'm not sure what he delivered, but he said he made five thousand dollars. He said it was just a note too." Sylvia continued. "Imagine someone paid him five thousand dollars just to deliver a note."

"Ms. Chase, that note he delivered was delivered to me." Rebecca held Sylvia's hand. "We need to know who paid January to deliver the note."

Sylvia reached for her phone and started to dial. "Hi Chase, it's your mother. I need your help really bad. Please hurry, I may need an ambulance." Sylvia was listening to what the voice on the other end was saying. "Thank you dear, see you soon." She hung up the phone and turned to the detective. "Detective Swanson, my son will be here in 5 minutes."

All four of them sat down and waiting what seemed like an eternity for the doorbell to ring. Finally after about 15 minutes they heard the buzzer. "Thank God I wasn't dying; I would have been dead by now." Sylvia buzzed him into the condo and again waited for him to show up. The 3 of them stood up and moved away from eye view of the door so he wouldn't flee. The door was unlocked and January opened it and walked into Sylvia's condo.

"Mom, I'm here! Are you alright?" He asked as Sylvia walked over to the door and locked it and blocking the entrance with her body.

"Yes, I'm alright, but I need you to talk to these people." Detective Swanson, Rebecca and Adam walked into view of January.

"Mom, you set me up? How could you?" January yelled at his mother.

"Sit your ass down. You're a big boy and if you did something wrong you have to pay!" His mother snapped back.

Detective Swanson walked behind January and was surprised he wasn't trying to flee. "January Chase, you're under arrest for an outstanding warrant for assault with a deadly weapon." The detective read him his Maranda Rights and hand cuffed him. He then brought him over to a chair and made him sit down. "You were visiting your mother the other day, we want to know who gave you that note you slipped under Miss Watson's door?"

January looked around the room and kept quiet. "Please, we need to know." Rebecca pleaded with him, and yet he still remained quiet.

Adam started to get frustrated with him. "Look you son of a bitch. You're being charged right now for miss a court date. We'll have the detective add 4 cases of assessor to 1st degree murder if you don't speak up. And remember, the state of Florida has the death penalty."

Whatever Adam said to him, it clicked that he's in bigger trouble than he was before. "Ok, I'll tell you. I don't remember his last name but his first name is David."

Rebecca and Adam looked at each other and simultaneously spoke. "David Waters?"

"Yes, that's him. David Waters." January started to talk like a parrot. "He gave me five thousand dollars to deliver an envelope to someone on the 30th floor. I had no idea what was in the envelope but when someone is paying five grand, you don't ask questions."

"That slimy piece of shit lied to me!" Rebecca said outload.

"Try to relax Rebecca. He doesn't know that we know he gave January the note. We're one step ahead of him." Adam said.

Detective Swanson took his cell phone out of his pocket and dials the station. "Hi, this is Detective Swanson. I need a uniformed Police officer to the7th floor of the Sun Rising Condo complex on Las Olas." He hung up the phone. "We'll wait for the officers to take Mr. Chase down to the station then pay a visit to our little friend David Waters."

There must have been a patrol car nearby since the officers showed up in 5 minutes. After they escorted him out of his mother's condo and the 3 of them left right behind thanking Ms. Chase for her help. "I bet the view from your condo is spectacular." Adam said. "I hope I'm able to see it some time."

Rebecca was thinking to her 'was he just flirting with me?' "Maybe after work we can go to that Italian restaurant and have a night cap at my place afterwards?" Rebecca was surprised how forward she was being. She never asked a guy out before, but it seemed so right with Adam.

"Sounds like a perfect plan. I can't wait!" Adam opened the car door for Rebecca and got into the car and drove to Dave Water's house again.

When the three of them arrived at the home of Mr. Waters they noticed the front door was opened. Detective Swanson signaled them to remain quiet as he snuck through the front door. After he entered the house he couldn't believe his eyes. David Waters was killed. Not just killed, but mutilated. He walked out and bent over the front stairs railing and started to vomit. Adam and Rebecca knew this couldn't be a good sign. The both of them started to walk towards the house. "I wouldn't go in there if I were you." The detective warned them.

There wasn't much Rebecca hadn't seen in her career at the F.B.I. As she and Adam walked in, they saw the carnage. David's body was mutilated. His arms and legs were torn off his torso. His head was severed also and placed on a broom handle. The blood was everywhere. When Rebecca looked up and seen the bloody writing on the wall. 'You guessed wrong' was written in blood. Her note said 'guess who' and now this clue.

CHAPTER 9

BACK TO SQUARE ONE

Back at the station Rebecca and Adam were looking for any clues in the photo's that the crime scene investigators took at Mr. Water's house. "I never saw so much blood in my life." Adam said putting down on of the photos. "I guess we're at square one again."

"I guess so, and after seeing that carnage, I don't think I'll be eating Italian anytime soon." Rebecca was trying to lighten the mood as she saw Adam smile. "Where's Detective Swanson?"

"I have no clue. The front desk told me that he'll be here." Adam looked at his watch and read that it was already 10AM. "Maybe he called in sick after throwing up at David's house?"

"Maybe he did call out, but unlikely. The guy is a professional." Just as Rebecca finished her sentence Detective Swanson walked into the conference room.

"Sorry I'm late, but I woke up with a damn flat tire." He said dropping his keys on the table. "Have you two figured out who did this yet?"

"Not quite, but I think we're getting close. He knew that we would go to January's home. He also knew that somehow he would spill the beans about Mr. Waters paying him to deliver the note. He's one step ahead of us." Rebecca picked up a piece of paper. "This is his bank record. There was twenty-five thousand dollars wired to his account the day that Mr. Chase was paid. The money came from an undisclosed source overseas so we can't trace the money."

"Great, so Mr. Waters were paid from an undisclosed overseas bank." Detective Swanson took a seat. "We're dealing with someone rich."

"That's what Rebecca and I were saying."

"There's only one thing left I can do." Rebecca said folding the file that was in her hands. "I have to go back to my home town in Massachusetts."

"Are you sure you want to do that Rebecca?" Adam asked concerned for her life. "There's a maniac lurking around, following your every footstep that you make."

"Ok, you guys have to hear me out. First of all I'm a former F.B.I. agent and know how to take care of myself. Secondly we have a profile on this guy. We know approximately his age so all I have to do is go through ten years of my high school yearbooks."

"Well Ms. Watson, I have no jurisdiction in Massachusetts so I doubt the department would fly me there to do an investigation that might lead to nowhere."

"Well Rebecca you're not going alone. I'm coming with you. I'm sure Mr. Thorton wouldn't mind." Adam picks up his cell phone and called Thorton Associates. "Hello, who is this speaking? Wendy, this is Adam May, would you please give Mr. Thorton a message for me? Tell him that Rebecca Watson and I are traveling to Boston for a few days for work." There was a slight pause. "She put me on hold. She's a temp filling in for Sharon." Adam returned to his call after being on hold for 5 minutes. "Thanks so much Wendy." He hung up his phone and turned to Rebecca. "So we're on the next flight to Boston and we're staying at the Four Season's Hotel on the Gardens." His phone vibrated and he looked down at his texts. "The flight leaves in 3 hours. Just enough time to throw a bag together and get to the airport."

"Well I guess that settles that problem. Adam, you're going to hate the city I grew up in." Rebecca said turning red because she was embarrassed of the city of Lynn.

"Well you two better get going. I'll call you if there are any new developments." Detective Swanson stood up and shook their hands for good luck. "I hope we narrow it down, and Rebecca, call me if you need anything."

"Will do detective, I'll call you if Adam and I find anything that could be a lead."

Both Rebecca and Adam left the police department and head to their homes to pack a bag. They both showed up at the airport on time before their scheduled flight was about to leave. The flight back to Boston would be approximately 3 ½ hours long. Rebecca needed to rest, she was exhausted. While on the flight Rebecca faded off to sleep and started to dream.

She was walking through the mall and nobody is there with her. She looks down and noticed she is walking in an inch of blood. Blood is everywhere she looks and bodies are floating by her. One body was faced up and she recognized her. The girl was her best friend Maggie. As she floated by Rebecca, Maggie's eyes opened and she spoke. "Help me Rebecca. Why did you do this to me Rebecca?" Rebecca started to run through the blood all the bodies started to mimic Maggie. "Help us Rebecca! Why did you do this to us?" All the strangers were grasping at her feet trying to stop her.

Rebecca came to the store where it all happened. There were no bodies to be found since they all just floated by her. Rebecca could make out a silhouette of a man standing there waiting for her. Rebecca started to walk closer to the man and she could finally see who the man was, it's her grandfather. She started to run towards her grandfather only to be stopped in her tracks by Dr. Peter Monteiro grabbing her arms. Rebecca started to scream. "Help me grandpa, help me!"

Rebecca looked at her grandfather walking away. She could hear him talking to her. "Let him kill you Rebecca. You'll save all these people lives." Rebecca started to see that all the people who were shot and killed that day line up behind her grandfather. They all started to chant. "Die Rebecca, die!" They chanted that over and over again. Dr. Monteiro was dragging her body through the river of blood. She looked up and saw the blade of a hunter's knife. He placed the knife to her throat. "Die bitch!" With one stroke of the knife the blade cut into her throat, spilling her blood with the rest of the people's blood. As she tried to stop the bleeding by holding her neck, she started to float in the blood and drifted by all the people that were killed. They were all pointing and laughing at her as she floated by. Some were chanting 'die Rebecca die!'

"Rebecca! Rebecca!"

Rebecca woke up in a pool of sweat. "Are you alight Rebecca?" Adam asked while shaking her shoulder to wake up.

"Yes, I'm alright. I was just having a terrible nightmare."

"I could tell that you were having a bad dream. You started to yell 'no, no, no'. Sorry I had to wake you up."

The airline attendant came over to Rebecca and gave her a clean wash cloth and a drink. "Here you go miss; I hope this will make you feel better."

"Thank you so much!" Rebecca took the wash cloth and wiped the sweat from her forehead and neck. She picked up the drink and took a sip. It was rum and coke, just what she needed to calm her nerves.

The pilot made his final approach announcement that they are about to land. As Rebecca and Adam departed the plane Rebecca heard a familiar voice. "Rebecca, over here honey!" The voice was her grandmother.

"Who is that?" Adam asked.

"That would be my grandmother." Rebecca replied as the two of them walked towards her grandmother. Rebecca was never fond of this woman. Unlike her father's parents, she was the mother of her mother. "Hi Gramma, how did you know I would be in Boston?"

Helen Rizzo was Rebecca's grandmother. She wasn't very nice to any of her grandchildren. She was a selfish, greedy, and hateful person. She was short and chunky with dyed auburn hair with gray roots showing. Her skin was prematurely wrinkled due to her chain smoking. At 58 she looked more like 78 and loved to drink vodka continuously. Her husband died and she now lives off his pension and she inherited a fortune from her family's business. Even though she was rich she never shared a single dime of her money. She never bought gifts for anyone, but always expected gifts for herself during the holidays or her birthday. Rebecca had really no use for her and she really didn't want to see her at the airport. "Gramma, my dear child, call me Helen. Gramma makes me sound so old. Who is this handsome gentleman?"

"Helen, this is my co-worker Adam May. Adam, this is my grandmother Helen."

"It's a pleasure meeting you ma'am." Adam said as he went in for a hug.

Helen backed away from him before he could touch her. "I'm sorry dear, but I'm not a hugging person."

Rebecca tried to distant herself from her. "Adam and I are here on business Helen. Again, how did you know I was going to be here today?"

"I received a text from somebody that told me you'll be coming to Boston for a few days. I just wanted to see my favorite granddaughter."

"Who sent you the text?" Rebecca asked as Helen showed her phone to her.

Rebecca took the phone out of Helen's hand. "How rude!"

"Hush woman!" Rebecca opened her phone and read the text from an anonymous sender.

Your granddaughter will be arriving at Logan Airport at 2PM. She'll be flying on American Airlines, flight #124. She'll be in Boston for a few days. She wants you to visit her. Dinner reservations have been made at Gilbert's Steak House in Boston for the 3 of you. The bill and tip has already been pre-paid. Have a great time!

Rebecca tried to call the number displayed on her phone only to get disconnected message. "Adam, only Detective Swanson, the temp at the office, and Mr. Thorton knew we were flying to Boston today. Why would anyone text a family member of mine telling them I'd be in Boston?"

"And why use a 'drop phone'? That worries me more than the fact someone texted your grandmother. They knew who to call, so they know your family." Adam was visibly worried for Rebecca. "This is getting too strange Rebecca. I really think you should go somewhere and hang low until we catch this bastard."

"That's not my style Adam." She whispered in his ear. "I'm a big girl; I know how to take care of myself."

"Excuse me?" Helen interrupted. "Are we going to dinner or what? There are reservations at Gilberts Steak House. The best part is it's already pre-paid!"

Helen loved free stuff, so it was easy to lure her into meeting Rebecca. "Grandma, I mean Helen; I think this is a trap. I'm here to investigate 5 murders that have happened in Fort Lauderdale area. I don't think it's a wise decision to go out with you tonight to a restaurant that we have no idea who made the reservations, or pre-paid for our meal. I want to call my boss to see if he had made the reservations before we even think about going."

Rebecca took out her business cell phone and called Mr. Thorton. "Hi, Mr. Thorton, it's Rebecca, I'm here in Boston with Adam and my grandmother received a text about having dinner reservations at a steak house call Gilberts. I was just wondering if you text her and made the reservations?" Helen and Adam heard the muffled voice on the other end of the phone talking to Rebecca. "Thanks so much Mr. Thorton." Rebecca turned to Adam and shook her head 'no'. "I'm sorry Helen; we're not going to Gilberts. My boss didn't make the reservations and I just don't think it's safe."

"That's just great! Thanks a lot Rebecca; I was counting on this dinner!" Helen seemed angry. "Enjoy your time in Boston!" Helen turned away and took off in a hurry since she wasn't getting a fee meal.

"Bye Grandma!" Rebecca yelled across the crowded airport so everyone could hear her. "Can you believe that woman?"

"It's alright Rebecca; we all have family members that suck." Adam hugged Rebecca like they were dating. "Well let's catch a cab and go to our hotel. We have a long day tomorrow at your old high school. What high school did you graduate from?"

"I went to Lynn Classical High." Rebecca answered. "And when you see my senior yearbook photo, you better not laugh!"

"I promise I won't laugh." Adam said while he was crossing his fingers.

The cab pulled up to the Four Season's Hotel where Rebecca and Adam had reservations. They walked into the lobby and were amazed how beautiful the place was decorated. They checked in and both received their room keys. Their rooms were situated right next to each other. Adam made sure of that in case there was a situation that occurred in Rebecca's room. "Well, good night Rebecca, see you in the AM."

Rebecca smiled at Adam. "Good night and thank you Adam for coming to Boston with me."

Adam just smiled back at Rebecca and entered his room. Rebecca shut her hotel room and took off her heals. Her feet were killing her and she needed to take a long hot bath. Rebecca called for room service and ordered a bottle of white wine and the chicken dinner that was on the hotel menu. Room service was extremely fast and there was a knock in the door within 15 minutes. Rebecca tipped the guy and poured herself a glass of wine. She tasted the chicken dinner that was served with roasted potatoes and asparagus. The chicken was cooked perfectly and she loved the hint of lemon she tasted. Rebecca's bathtub was just about full. Rebecca undressed and took her wine and sat in the hot bath water to sooth her aches and pains.

Rebecca must have stayed in the bathtub for over an hour and was well relaxed and ready to lie down in her bed and watch the television. She turned on the T.V. and changed the channel to the news network. Rebecca loved being informed and loved how CNN gave her all the news that was true, unlike Fox News that likes to spread lies and report misinformation.

Helen, being as thrifty as she was, wasn't going to let a free meal go to waste. She drove to Boston and parked her car in front of Gilbert's Steak House and entered the restaurant. The Matradee at Gilberts greeted her with a smile. "Does my lady have a reservation?" He asked politely.

"Yes, it should be under Rebecca Watson." Helen hoped it was under her name since she totally forgot that Adam's last name was May.

"Yes, Ms. Watson, will the other 2 be joining your party shortly?"

"They should be here momentarily." The matradee escorted Helen to her table and pulled out her chair. When she was seated, he took the napkin off the table and placed it on her lap. "Thank you young man."

The Matradee handed her the menu and the wine list. Helen looked over the menu and figured since she wasn't paying for it, she might as well go big. The waitress walked over to Helen. "Are you ready to order Miss?"

"Yes, I'll have the most expensive bottle of your merlot wine. I'll start by having the garden salad with creamy Italian dressing. For my main course I'll have the baked stuffed lobster, stuffed with lobster." Helen closed the menu and handed them to the waitress.

The waitress brought back a bottle of wine that costed over 300 dollars. She poured a little into Helens glass. Like a pro, Helen swirled the wine in her glass and smelled it before taking a sip of the wine. "That's perfect dear." The waitress poured the rest of the wine into the glass filling it half way. Not too long after she was served her salad and dinner. She was eating like a king and laughed a little that Rebecca and Adam didn't take advantage of the free dinner.

After dinner was over, the waitress brought over the dessert cart and Helen picked out the baked Alaska. Helen waited for her dessert to arrive and another waiter approached her. "Excuse me Ma'am, are you Rebecca Watson?"

Helen knew she had to keep up the charade. "Why yes young man, I am Rebecca Watson."

The waiter planted a big box in front of Helen. "This was delivered for you Ma'am."

Helen looked excited. Whoever paid for this dinner now sent Rebecca an elaborate present. The box was beautifully decorated with silver wrapping paper and a silk bow. Helen knew she shouldn't open the box, but her curiosity overcame her. Helen started to remove the bow slowly so she wouldn't ruin it. She knew she could re-use it for a gift in the future. She accidently tore the paper so she just ripped the rest of the paper off the rest of the gift. There were no markings on the box that could reveal what was inside, so Helen picked it up and tried to shake it. The contents didn't move so the only way she would know was to open it gift. She took her butter knife and cracked the seal. She slowly opened the box. A bright flash of light burnt her eyes.

Boom!

CHAPTER 10

I FALL TO PIECES

Rebecca was lying in her bed listening to radio as Patsy Cline was singing 'I Fall to Pieces' when she seen the breaking news flash on the T.V. Rebecca lowered the radio and turned the volume up on the television to hear what the reporter had to say.

An explosion occurred at Gilberts Steak House around 7pm tonight. Police and Fire have been called to the scene. The cause of the explosion has not been determined. There is rubble everywhere and there are no signs of survivors. We'll update you soon as this story develops.

Rebecca jumped out of bed and opened the connecting door to Adams room. Adam simultaneously opened his side of the door and both spoke at the same time. "Did you hear the news?"

"Have you talked with your grandmother? Do you think she would have gone there for dinner?" Adam asked since he was truly concerned about Helen.

Rebecca picked up the phone and dialed her grandmother's number. "There's no answer. I think she went there to eat since it was free." Rebecca started getting dressed in front of Adam. At this point she didn't care if Adam seen her naked or not. "I'm going down to the F.B.I headquarters and then to Gilbert's restaurant."

Adam ran into his room. "Not without me. I'm going with you, but I have to ask, why are we going to the F.B.I?"

"I want my badge back so I can have more power to investigate all these killings. Detective Swanson is doing as good as he can, but he's not able to do a lot of things an F.B.I agent can do."

Rebecca and Adam left the hotel and went directly to the Boston F.B.I. Headquarters. The director of the Boston branch met with both of them while they explained the situation. Deputy Director Thomas knew Rebecca well and was sad to see her leave the F.B.I. to work for Thorton Associates.

Philip Thomas was a 40 year veteran of the bureau and loved his job. He was a tall thin man with gray hair, mustache and beard. The whites of his eyes were turning yellow with age and a golden brown tint lined his mustache from all the cigarettes he smoked. He became the director of the Boston branch 10 years ago after he told his director he was retiring. He convinced Thomas to stay and a few weeks later he was promoted to director after the sudden death of his boss. Thomas' blue eyes have seen a lot in his 40 years of service. He was shot and nearly died on the job 15 years ago. Thomas sat behind his desk and listened to Rebecca and Adam and all the evidence they had that the bombing could be related to all the murders in Fort Lauderdale. "Well, it's great to have you back on the force even though it's just for a few weeks. Thomas reached into his desk and took out Rebecca's old badge and gun and handed it to her. "I knew you'd be back. I just didn't think it would be this soon." Rebecca took her badge and gun and thanked the director for understanding the situation. "If anyone can catch this guy, it's you Rebecca. Good luck!"

Rebecca and Adam raced to the scene of the explosion. The street where the restaurant was once standing was blocked off by police cars and fire apparatus'. Rebecca showed the police officer her badge and asked who was in charge of the scene. The officer pointed out a plain clothed officer who was taking notes. "Excuse me, are you in charge?" Rebecca showed him her credentials.

The guy looked at her badge and yelled out loud. "Who called the fucking feds?"

The guy seemed agitated that Rebecca was going to take over his investigation. "I'm Rebecca Watson and this is my co-worker Adam May. Nobody called the fucking F.B.I. I saw what happened on the news and came over. My Grandmother might have been in the restaurant at the time of the explosion."

The guy was an asshole. He came across arrogant and didn't like females that had a higher position than he had. He wore regular street clothes, t-shirt and jeans. The guy wasn't tall and stood about 5 feet 5 inches. He was balding and his hair was a mess. Rebecca thought he looked just like Danny DeVito. "Are there any survivors Detective?" Rebecca paused and asked him his name.

"Detective Patrick Quinlan." He responded.

"Well Detective Quinlan, are there any survivors?" She asked.

"There was one survivor, an older woman, 60ish. She's in the ambulance being prepped to be taken to the hospital. I highly doubt she'll survive her injuries." Detective Quinlan pointed to the ambulance where the victim was being treated.

Adam ran over to the ambulance and looked at the badly burnt woman who was missing both her legs and her left arm from the explosion. "Is she alert?"

"She's barley alive, but you can try to talk to her." The medic sat back and let Adam get closer to the victim. He knew instantly that it was Helen, Rebecca's grandmother.

Adam held her hand. "Helen, it's me Adam." Helen opened her eyelids only to reveal that one eye was blown out of her socket. Her hair was burnt to her skull.

In a very weak voice Helen tried to talk. "Adam. The box was addressed to Becky."

Helen became unresponsive. Adam moved away as the medics tried frantically to save her life. Adam looked at the heart monitor and saw that it went flat line. Helen had died from her injuries, and Adam knew she was better off dead. Adam walked out of the ambulance and stopped Rebecca from going inside. "It was your grandmother Rebecca. You don't want to see her in that condition. It's too late Rebecca, she's gone." The doors of the ambulance closed and started to drive off. "Before she died Rebecca, she said something about a package addressed to you."

"Dear God, who is doing this to me Adam?" Rebecca put her head on his chest and Adam squeezed her. "Why don't they just come after me, why do they have to kill everyone I know?"

Adam brushed her hair gentle whit his hand. "We'll find him Rebecca, if that's the last thing I do, we'll find the bastard!"

Adam and Rebecca left the scene and went back to the hotel. Rebecca called her old school and talked with the principal. "Hello, my name is Rebecca Watson; I'm an F.B.I. agent investigating multiple murders. I need you to send me copies of all the yearbooks from 2008 through 2018." Rebecca gave the man on the other end the address to Thorton Associates where they can send the books. "Thank you very much." Rebecca hung up the phone. "The yearbooks will be arriving in 2 days."

Adam poured Rebecca a drink from the mini bar. "Here drink this it'll calm your nerves." Rebecca took the glass from Adam and started to drink the rum and coke he prepared. Rebecca sat on the edge of her bed and Adam sat next to her. "Are you alright?"

"I'll be fine Adam." Rebecca looked into Adams eyes and just gazed at him. "You are so handsome." Rebecca realized she just said that out loud. "Oh my God Adam, I'm sorry. I didn't mean to say that."

Adam put his fingers to Rebecca's mouth to quiet her. "Don't be sorry Rebecca, I find you very beautiful." Adam leaned and started to kiss Rebecca's mouth. They both liked each other and the sexual attraction finally took over.

Rebecca and Adam laid on the bed and started to remove each other's clothing. "Oh Adam!" Rebecca whispered into his ear. The both of them rolled around the bed in their under garments and were passionately making out. They were going hot and heavy and Rebecca suddenly stopped. "I can't Adam, I can't do this."

"What's wrong? We both find each other attractive and I have feelings for you." Adam said kissing her neck.

Rebecca pushed Adam away and got out of the bed. "Adam, anyone who gets close to me ends up dead. I can't have you dying on me."

Adam walked behind Rebecca and moved his hands down from her shoulders to her hands. "I understand Rebecca." Adam bent over and picked up his clothing and started to walk out of Rebecca's hotel room. "I'll be right next door if you need me. I'll keep my side of the door open." Adam walked out and closed Rebecca's door on her side.

"Thank you Adam for understanding." Rebecca said as she closed the door behind him and lay down on her bed.

CHAPTER 11

ANOTHER BITES THE DUST

Rebecca and Adam took an early flight back to Ft. Lauderdale. They both decided to take a day off to recuperate from the terrible explosion that occurred in Boston. As they sat in the back of an Uber car, Rebecca turned to Adam. "Do you think we'll catch this bastard?"

Adam looked deep into Rebecca's eyes and gently kissed her soft velvet lips. "I know we'll catch him!" Adam smiled at her as the car came to a stop. "Well, guess this is your stop. Go get some rest and I'll call you later. Would you like to have dinner with me?"

"Are you going to show up this time?" Rebecca asked jokingly. "Let's meet at Bistro Mezzaluna. I really liked their food, and they make a great vodka Martini."

"It's a date and I promise I won't stand you up this time." Adam kissed Rebecca on the cheek and waved goodbye to her as she left the car. There was no doubt that there was an attraction between Adam and Rebecca.

Rebecca walked into her condo and sat down on her bed. She was exhausted from all the drama that just happened in Boston. Even though Rebecca really didn't care about her grandmother, she still was upset that she was killed in the explosion.

Her boss at Thorton Associates had no idea that she was re-instated as an F.B.I. agent. She hoped that Willard would understand why she was 'moonlighting'. She knew that now she has her credentials back, she would be able to obtain more information about the case with the Fort Lauderdale police department. Rebecca would worry about telling Willard tomorrow about being back at the F.B.I. She will explain to Willard that she wasn't getting paid by the F.B.I. so it wouldn't interfere with her job at Thorton Associates.

Rebecca undressed and laid in her bed. She drifted off to sleep really fast since she was dead tired. Rebecca started to dream and she became restless in her sleep. She was tossing and turning. The images of all those innocent people came back to haunt her. The blood was dripping down their necks as they approached her slowly. They were chanting 'Rebecca' over and over again. Their voices were gargling with the blood. They were like zombies but they could talk. They surrounded Rebecca and started to pull her in two different ways. Her arms were being pulled to the point of being dislocated. She heard her skin tearing and she was screaming with pain. She couldn't stop them; they had death in their eyes. She was responsible for them being dead and they're getting their revenge.

Rebecca was woken up with a bang on the door. She looked at her clock that was beside her bed. "Who could be knocking on my door at 3 in the morning?" Rebecca threw on a robe and walked over to the door. She knew whoever was knocking the news wasn't going to be good. She looked through her peep hole and saw that it was Detective Swanson banging at her door. Rebecca opened the door. "Detective, do you know what time it is?"

"I'm sorry that I woke you up Rebecca. Could you get dressed? I need you at a crime scene."

Without asking, Rebecca went to her bedroom and threw on a pair of jeans, a t-shirt, and her sneakers. "Ready when you are Detective."

Detective Swanson lead Rebecca to the elevator. "Where are we going?" Rebecca asked.

"You'll see." Detective Swanson pressed the 7th floor elevator button.

"Are we going to Mrs. Chase's condo?" Rebecca had a real bad feeling about what she was about to encounter.

Rebecca walked out of elevator on to the 7th floor. She noticed a bunch of cops standing in the hallway just talking. Then she saw the yellow crime scene tape blocking off the entrance to Sylvia Chase's condo. As she walked towards the unit that Sylvia lived in, she could feel all eyes on her. "Does anyone have any gloves?" She asked. A uniformed officer walked over and gave her a pair of gloves. Rebecca places the gloves on her hands so that she didn't ruin any evidence that maybe inside the unit. The officer handed her some shoe covering. "You may need these." Rebecca looked puzzled and opened the unit's door. As she walked in, she saw the blood shed that occurred in the unit.

"Oh my fucking God!" Rebecca said as she couldn't believe her eyes. "This can't be the same killer. There are body parts everywhere. Our killer only slices their necks."

"I think it is our guy. Come look in the bedroom." Detective Swanson lead Rebecca to the bedroom. There in the bed were Sylvia's and January's head on the pillows. Above the bed there was 'Rebecca' written in blood. "Whoever did this to them knew we spoke with January." The detective turned around to face Rebecca. "I'm worried about you Rebecca. I heard what happened in Boston. That could have been you in that restaurant."

Rebecca knew that he was right. Whoever was doing these killings was now a threat to her. "He's playing a cat and mouse game. He wants me to play with him."

"Did you find anything out while you were in Boston?" The detective asked.

"Unfortunately Adam and I didn't have time to go to my high school to check out the year books. I know the answer has to be in one of those books. The school is sending me 10 years of books for me to go through. I'm hoping they arrive tomorrow." Rebecca looked at her phone to see the time. "I mean they're arriving today." Rebecca wasn't use to being waken up at 3 in the morning. "By the way, I've been re-instated by the F.B.I."

"That's great news! Will we have access to their lab?"

"I'm sure we'll be able to use their lab and data base. I'm going to the Miami base office and do some cross referencing to see if there are any similar cases." Rebecca had seen enough of the latest crime scene and started to exit out of the condo. "Detective, make sure you dust for any prints. Take samples of all the blood splatter, especially the writing on the wall. We need a finger print match, or we'll never get a lead on this case."

Rebecca left the condo and entered the elevator to her unit on the 30th floor. She entered her unit and turned on the television and started to watch the news as she brewed a fresh cup of coffee. Rebecca sat on the couch and drank her coffee. She loved her new apartment, especially the 85 inch television set mounted on the wall. She had a television in every room. The bedroom had a 55 inch television, and even the bathroom had a 40 inch TV to watch while taking a bath in her soaking tub. As she was watching they started to report from Lynn, Massachusetts. Rebecca took the remote and turned up the volume.

"We're here in Lynn, Massachusetts where there has been several major fires burning at the same time. We're standing in front of one of those fires. Behind me is Lynn Classical High School. This has been burning since last night. As you can see multiple fire units from all over the state are fighting this blaze. Five other structures are burning also, and those fires have been started approximately the same time. The city of Lynn's fire chief told us that all the buildings were vacant and no injuries have been reported thus far. The other burning buildings include City Hall, Lynn English High School, Simons a human body fluid storage facility, the Lynn Public Library, and one home on Western Ave and the other on Eastern Ave. Currently the fire and police have no suspects involved in these fires. However, they assume this was arson." The reporter held her hand to her ear. "I just got word from the producers, that a woman was killed in the Western Ave home fire. Her name isn't being released until the family of the victim has been notified. I'm Victoria Reynolds reporting for WHCV news."

Rebecca couldn't believe what she was witnessing on TV. Her old high school was burning to the ground. Before the camera went back to the news room, she noticed some graffiti on the wall of the school. Written in huge red letters was her name. She needs to know if it was just a coincidence. She called the Lynn police department and asked for the chief of police. "Good morning, this is Rebecca Watson from the F.B.I."

The officer over the phone sounded young. "No problem Agent Watson let me transfer you to the captain on duty. The chief doesn't arrive on duty until 9am."

"Hello, this is Captain Collins, how may I help you Agent Watson?"

"Captain, I'm working on a case down here in Ft. Lauderdale that I may need some information from you. I saw on TV that 5 major building are burning at the same exact time. Though the news station down here only reported from the Lynn Classical building I noticed that the word 'Rebecca' was written on the wall of the high school." Rebecca paused and decided not to tell him her name was Rebecca. "I need to know if the other buildings have been vandalized with graffiti. Could you please check on that for me and call me back?"

"No problem Agent Watson. Is the phone number on my caller ID correct? Is that the best way to contact you?"

"Yes, and I don't want to be pushy, but could call me as soon as possible?" Rebecca needed to know if all those fires were deliberately set because she was getting close to her assailment.

"I'll get right on it Agent Watson."

"Thank you Captain, I really appreciate it. I'll talk with you later." Rebecca hung up the phone and looked at the clock on the wall. "It's 5am way too early to call Adam. Especially since we're taking today off from the investigation." Rebecca walked into her bedroom to take a nap since she's been up since 3 in the morning.

Rebecca woke up 3 hours later at 8am. She got out of her bed and walked into the bathroom to take a shower. As she was showering her phone rang. She didn't hear it ring since her head was under the shower head and the water was making her deaf to any sounds around her. She dried off and got dressed for the day. She only wore a white t-shirt and a pair of shorts made out of denim. She picked up the phone and noticed the miss call. She automatically dialed her voice mail.

"Hi Rebecca its Adam, call me when you get a chance."

"Why do I always get calls when I'm busy?" Rebecca dialed Adam's number. "Good morning Adam, I was in the shower when you called. What's going on?"

"Nothing much going on, I was just checking in on you to see if you were doing alright."

Rebecca thought that was a sweet gesture. "I'm alright Adam, thanks for asking. However, did you hear the news?"

"No, I just woke up a few minutes ago. I haven't had time to really relax and have my coffee. What's going on?" Adam asked.

"First there was a double murder in my building. January Chase and his mother Sylvia was found mutilated in her unit. My name was written on her bedroom wall." Rebecca continued. "I also saw on the news this morning several major fires were burning in my home city. The high school I went too was burning to the ground and Adam; I saw my name in big letters on the wall of the building. Did he know I was requesting the year books?"

"Holy shit Rebecca, you have to leave your condo. You're in too much danger. Why don't you stay with me until this is all over?"

"Can we speak of this during dinner Adam?" Rebecca asked politely. "I really don't want to run from this guy. I'm ok with being the bait Adam. I think it's the only way to catch this son of a bitch!"

Adam remained quiet for a few seconds trying to figure out a way to convince her to stay with him. "Alright Rebecca we'll talk about it over dinner. I do respect your decision even though I think it's the wrong choice."

"Thank you Adam for understanding. I'll see you tonight at Mezzaluna around 7pm. Talk to you later. Bye." Adam said bye and Rebecca hung up her phone. She was hoping that the books were sent out to her before the fire started. She really wanted to go through the books today.

Rebecca left her condo and headed to her office to see if the books arrived. She entered her office to find several big boxes that were shipped to her by FedEx. The return address was Lynn Classical High. "Thank you dear Jesus for getting these books to me before the fire." There were 4 big boxes and Rebecca decided to take them to her car. She only could carry one at a time since the boxes were heavy. "How many books did they send me?" Rebecca placed on of the boxes into her car and started to take the elevator back to her office floor.

While on the elevator, Rebecca heard a huge explosion coming from the garage. The elevator shook violently and started to fall due to the explosion. Rebecca braced herself for impact when the elevator hit the ground. Luckily the elevator stopped right before impact. Rebecca was tossed to the floor, but she wasn't hurt. She stood up and dusted herself off. She pried opened the elevator doors and seen she was back in the basement garage. There was no big damage to the garage but her car was on fire from the explosion. The box she placed in her car was a bomb. She stood there stunned as she was thinking that the device could have gone off in the elevator as she was bringing it down.

Rebecca heard the fire trucks approaching. The sirens could be heard for miles. The fire trucks were escorted by the police department. One of the officers approached Rebecca. "Are you alright Miss?" Rebecca nodded to the officer that she was alright. "Well let's get you checked out by the paramedics just to be sure." The officer led Rebecca out of the garage and into the back of the ambulance.

As the paramedics were looking after her Detective Swanson came running over to her. "Are you alright Miss Watson?"

"Yes I'm alright; I just fell when the elevator came to a stop before hitting the ground."

As She was about to tell him what happened, another explosion occurred on the 17th floor right where Rebecca's office was. Glass was hailing down on the people below as the fire department rushed to the building where the explosion had occurred. "That's my office!" Rebecca yelled.

"What's going on Miss Watson? Have you figured anything out yet?" The detective now wanted answers from Rebecca. "You're the target of everything that has been going on lately."

Rebecca knew the detective was right. She was the target now. "I received 4 big boxes from my old high school today. I hope nobody was hurt."

"What was in those boxes Miss Watson?"

"They were supposed to be high school yearbooks from my old school. Now they've been all destroyed."

"Why don't you just call your old high school again and get them to send you another copy?"

Rebecca looked into the detectives eyes. "Did you watch the news this morning? My school burned down with 4 other buildings in Lynn. And I think all the fires have something to do with the suspect." Rebecca's cell phone started to ring. It was Adam. "Hello?"

"Rebecca I just heard what happen. Mr. Thorton sent out a text message about the explosions that took place at work. Thank god nobody was injured. I'm glad we both took today off."

Rebecca didn't want Adam to worry about her, so she told him a little lie. "I know it's terrible. Thank God we weren't at work. Unfortunately all the year books have been destroyed in the explosion. I received a notice of delivery right before it happened. The bomb must have been in one of the boxes delivered to me." Rebecca felt bad about lying to him, and she knew she would have to come clean at dinner time when she showed up without her car. We have a lot to talk about at dinner. I'll see you later, and Adam, thank you for caring."

Rebecca stood up and she started to get dizzy. Her equilibrium was thrown off from the elevator drop. "Are you alright Miss Watson?" The detective asked as he seen her stumble.

"I'll be fine, but could you give me a ride home. My car looks like it won't be running for a while." Rebecca smiled since she knew nobody was injured in the blast.

"I'll give you a lift home Miss Watson." The detective offered her a ride and Rebecca accepted.

As the detective was driving her home he had to tell her something that she might not want to hear. "Miss Watson, I hate to do this to you, but I'm calling Mr. Thorton and taking you off the case. It's becoming too personal for you and he or she is coming after you."

Rebecca knew deep down that the detective was right. It was getting too personal for her to continue, but she also knew that she was the best profiler in the business. If anyone could figure out who's behind these killings, it would be her. "Do what you have to do Detective; I've been re-instated by the F.B.I. So I'll continue the investigation myself with the Bureau."

Rebecca was adamant what she wanted to do, and that was to stay on the case. "Detective, who else would be good bait besides me, after all he is coming after me."

"Miss Watson, I'm supposed to uphold the law and protect the citizens of Fort Lauderdale. I would be breaking my oath if I let you be bait."

The detective pulled in front of Rebecca's condo unit and Rebecca got out of the car. "Thanks for the lift Detective. You're either with me or I do this alone!" Rebecca made her deal and she was firmly sticking by her decision.

"You're a stubborn one Miss Watson." The detective was shaking his head in disgust. "Alright, see you at the station at 9. We'll figure this out together."

Rebecca smiled at the detective. "Thanks, I'll be there on time."

Rebecca entered her condo and sat on the couch. Her eyes were getting heavy since she was awakening at 3am by the detective. She closed her eyes and faded off to sleep.

Rebecca woke up from her extend nap just in time to get ready for dinner with Adam. Rebecca didn't know what to wear and finally picked out a gorgeous blue dress that fit her like a glove. Rebecca thought about Adam a lot lately and she finally admitted to herself that she was attractive to him. She was worried about one thing and one thing only, and that was the fact he was her co-worker. Rebecca never dated anyone from work. She always had one rule, don't shit where you eat. But she thought about her rule and figured it to be silly. She knew the risks and she wanted to take them. Plus, Adam was a great profiler himself and could help Rebecca figure out a plan to catch this killer.

Rebecca looked in the mirror and was dressed to kill. She looked beautiful and she knew Adam would like it. Rebecca left her condo and took an Uber to the restaurant. Standing outside waiting for her was none other than Adam. Adam walked over to the car and opened the door for her. "What happened to your car?"

Rebecca smiled at him and kissed him on the cheek. "It's a long story, I'll explain over dinner. I'm starving!"

CHAPTER 12

AFTER DINNER DESSERT

Rebecca woke up the next morning with the biggest smile on her face. Lying next to her was Adam. Both of them were naked and she couldn't help herself admiring Adams body. She took her hand and ran her fingers down his neck to his six pack abs. Rebecca knew he might be good in bed, but she never imagined him being great.

Rebecca started to reminisce about what happened last night. The evening started out normal, like two co-workers having dinner and talking about work. "Adam, I have to tell you that I lied to you this morning. I was at the office when my car and office exploded." Rebecca looked at Adam with puppy dog eyes.

"I knew you were lying to me from get go. I also know you didn't want to tell me because I would have been worried about you." Adam reached over the table and held her hand. "I am worried about you Rebecca, because I like you, and I care about you."

Rebecca and Adam looked in each other eyes and knew there was chemistry between the two. Rebecca's rule of don't shit where you eat was about to be thrown out the window. Rebecca took a sip of her martini to get the courage to tell him how she felt. "Adam." Before she could say anything the waiter interrupted her.

"Are you ready to order?" The waiter looked like he belonged in grade school. He looked way too young to be a waiter. "Does the lady know what she'll be having tonight?" He asked while tapping his pen on the order pad that was in his hand.

"I'll have the linguini and seafood combination." Rebecca responded.

"Excellent decision, and what would the gentleman like order tonight?"

"I'll have what she's having." Adam closed his menu and handed it back to the waiter. "May I also have a bottle of your best cabernet?"

"Yes sir, I'll be right back with your order." The waiter took Rebecca's menu and walked away to place their orders.

"What were you about to say before you were interrupted?"

"It can wait until after dinner." Rebecca paused and wiped her lips with her napkin. "I do have to tell you that the year book route we were going to investigate was destroyed in the explosion. Now that the school burnt down and the library they'll be impossible to get."

"We'll figure something out Rebecca."

The waiter returned to the table with a bottle of cabernet and poured a little into Adam's glass. Adam looked like a wine connoisseur the way he handled the wine. Adam swirled the wine in his glass and sniffed the bouquet. He then proceeded to take a sip of the wine. "This is an excellent choice of wine young man." With Adam's approval the waiter began to pour the wine into their glasses. Adam lifted his glass and made a toast. "To finding whoever the killer could be!" Rebecca and Adam clanked glasses and took a sip of the wine.

"This is excellent wine." Rebecca said while taking another sip. "So what should we do about the yearbooks?"

Adam thought about the question for a few moments. "What about the Library of Congress? Would they have a copy of the books?"

"Adam, that's a brilliant idea. All publications are stored at the Library of Congress. I'll make a call to them tomorrow. Maybe you and I can take a trip to the Capital?" Rebecca paused. "I'm sure Mr. Thorton would approve of the trip. Would you ask him since you have seniority?"

"That'll be no problem Rebecca. You call the library and I'll call Mr. Thorton." They both lifted their glass and drank on the proposal they just made.

Rebecca and Adam were laughing and enjoying each other's company. Rebecca hadn't had this much fun since the night she went to George's Alibi. Adam ordered another bottle of wine and Rebecca was getting a little light headed from the alcohol. "Look at the time Adam." Rebecca said looking at her cell phone. "It's close to midnight. I really should call it a night." Rebecca picked up her phone and started to open the app for Uber.

"What are you doing Rebecca?" Adam asked. "Close that app, I'll drive you home."

Rebecca just smiled at him and agreed to let him drive her home. The waiter walked over and placed the bill in front of Adam. "How much do I owe Adam?"

"Dinner is on me. It's not often I have the pleasure of a beautiful woman joining me for dinner."

Rebecca started to scrimmage though her purse to get some money out. "Thank you for dinner Adam, but I'll leave the tip."

The two of them left the restaurant and started to drive to Rebecca's condo. The two of them just sat there with an awkward silence between the two of them. Adam stopped his car in front of Rebecca's building. Every time Rebecca looked at Adam lately, her heart melted. She was more than fond of him; she thought she was actually falling in love with him. "Would you like to come up for a night cap Adam?"

Adam smiled at her and nodded yes. "Are you sure Rebecca?"

Rebecca Boldly reached over and took his car keys out of the ignition. "Now you really don't have a choice do you?" She was grinning ear to ear as she got out of the car.

"I guess I don't have a choice." Adam giggled a little and followed her into the lobby of her building.

The two of them entered the elevator and Rebecca pressed the 30th floor button. As soon as the doors closed Rebecca turned to Adam and planted a sweet gentle kiss. The kiss took Adam by a surprise, but he didn't push her away. The two of them started to get hot and heavy in the elevator. Adam turned Rebecca around and pressed her against the wall. Rebecca wrapped her left leg around Adam so he couldn't escape. Rebecca slid her tongue into

Adam's mouth and Adam copied her move. They were going at it so hot they almost didn't make it to Rebecca's condo dressed.

Once they reached her condo, Rebecca shut the door behind him. She took his hand and led him to the bedroom. The kissing slowed down to a gentle passionate mode. Adam started to kiss Rebecca's neck and slid his tongue down to where her dress met her neck. He slowly unzipped the back of her dress as Rebecca was unbuttoning his shirt. Rebecca marveled how chiseled his torso was and began unbuckling his belt buckle. Rebecca moved her arms so Adam could gently remove her dress. He was bringing the dress down and moving his tongue down her body as the dress fell to the floor.

They were both standing naked in front of each other and Adam moved in and started to kiss Rebecca's lips while he moved his hand to caress her breast. Adam led Rebecca to the bed and they both lay down together. Rebecca moved her hand and cradled Adams penis. As she held his cock in her hand it grew and grew. Rebecca thought that it would never stop growing. Adam was very well hung, at least 11 inches hard. Adam removed Rebecca's hand as he started to lick every square inch of her body. He took her breast and started to lick and suck on each nipple like a new born baby. Rebecca moaned with pleasure. He started to go south with his tongue and stopped at her thighs. He marveled at the sight of her pussy, and loved the fact she was completely shaved.

Adam placed a finger into her pussy and started to finger fuck her until she was nice and moist. Adam had a long tongue and started to lick the inside of her pussy. He knew how to orally service a woman, and he knew by the way Rebecca was reacting that he was doing a great job.

"Oh, Adam, that feels so good. Please don't stop!" Rebecca said as she was squirming around in the bed.

Adam started to add another finger into her pussy using 2 fingers while he licked her clitoris. Adam stopped and whispered into Rebecca's ear. "Do you want my cock?"

Rebecca started to French kiss Adam as she muttered 'yes'. "I want you deep in me Adam!"

Adam guided his cock into Rebecca's pussy slowly so she could get use to the size. "Go deeper Adam, Deeper!" Adam was eager to oblige to fill her with his manhood. Adam started to thrust slowly as Rebecca dug her nails into his back. Adam started to fuck her harder and harder. He looked down to see Rebecca's eyes closed while she licked her own lips. Adam knew she was enjoying his cock so he started to thrust hard. He was close to ejaculate. "I'm going to cum!"

"I want to feel you cum in me!" Rebecca screamed.

Adam fucked faster and faster as sweat poured from his back and forehead. "I'm cumming!" Adam screamed. Adam exploded his seed deep into Rebecca's pussy. He held his position until he was done. Adam pulled his cock out of her pussy and rolled over with exhaustion. Rebecca placed her hands on Adam's chest and then slid down to take his huge cock into her mouth. She loved the taste of his seamen as she stroked the last drop out of him. After she was done cleaning his cock, Rebecca fell into his arms. "Fuck Adam, that was terrific!" She smiled at him and kissed him gently.

"I'm glad that you enjoyed it Rebecca." Adam stroked Rebecca's long blond hair as they both fell asleep in each other's arms.

Rebecca stopped day dreaming about what happened the night before when Adam spoke. "Good morning beautiful. I hope you slept well." Adam kissed Rebecca softly on the cheek.

"Good morning handsome. Thank you so much for dinner and the delicious dessert afterwards." Rebecca rolled out of bed naked and started to walk into the shower.

"Where are you going?"

"I'm going to take a shower. I have a flight to Washington D.C. remember?"

"Holy shit, I totally forgot our conversation last night." Adam said as he wacked his own forehead.

Rebecca started to laugh. "Well I hope you don't forget what we did last night."

Adam rolled out of the bed and walked over to Rebecca. "I will never forget what we did last night." Adam kissed her and they started to make out. Rebecca saw that Adam was getting an erection again.

"Stop Adam, we can't do another round just yet. Let's wait until I get back from Washington." Rebecca slapped Adam's firm ass and walked into the bathroom to shower.

Adam gathered his clothes that were thrown everywhere, from the living room to the bedroom. He got dressed and wrote Rebecca a note before he left and left it on her pillow.

Rebecca got out of the shower and noticed the note on her pillow and read it out loud. "Dear Rebecca, Thank you so much for the best night of my life. I thought you were beautiful when I first met you, and now I think I'm falling for you, Adam." Rebecca held the note to her bare breast and placed it on her dresser. She got dressed and headed to the airport to catch her flight to D.C.

CHAPTER 13

CHAOS

Rebecca's flight arrived 4 hours late due to the thunder storms happening in D.C. She wasn't happy at all since she just wasted the whole day traveling. After she left the terminal and arrived at her hotel she called Adam.

The phone kept ringing. "Come on Adam, pick up the fucking phone." Adam never picked up and Rebecca left a message on his voice mail. "Hey Adam, it's me, Rebecca. I just got to my hotel room here in D.C. Call me when you get a chance."

Rebecca hung up the phone and started to pace. She was nervous that something terrible might have happened to Adam. She already lost so many people close to her being killed because of their association with her. Wild visions of Adam being found dead with his neck slashed really worried her.

Rebecca's cell phone started to ring. She looked at the number and she didn't recognize it. "Hello."

"Good evening, is this Miss Rebecca Watson?"

"This is Rebecca; may I ask whose calling?"

"Miss Watson, this is Wendy Sullivan from the Ft. Lauderdale coroner's office."

Rebecca's heart started to break. She started to shake since any calls from the coroner's office weren't going to be good news. "Is this about Adam May?"

"No Miss Watson, this is about Sylvia and January Chase."

Rebecca felt relieved. "How may I help you?"

"Well I just wanted to give you an update on the autopsy. We came to the conclusion that both Sylvia and January wasn't dead before their heads were cut off. Both were tortured violently. After their limbs were cut off with a dull object and afterwards a tunicate was placed on their limbs to keep them alive."

"Do you know what type of instrument was used to remove their limbs?"

"The victim's limbs were removed by a very dull ordinary hand tooth saw. Both of them suffered dearly. I've never seen anything like it before."

Rebecca took in what Wendy was saying. "Thank you Wendy for calling."

Rebecca hung up the phone and felt relieved that Adam wasn't dead. Then she thought how disgusting it was the way they were killed. "Whoever did this wanted them to suffer. I can understand January being killed for talking to us, but I can't understand why they killed Sylvia."

Rebecca tried calling Adam again and this time he finally picked up. "Jesus Christ Adam, you had me worried sick."

"I'm terribly sorry, but I was in a meeting with Mr. Thorton on what we were doing. He totally agreed and will be paying for your transportation and hotel."

"It's alright, I understand, but everyone who gets close to me ends up dying." Rebecca went on to tell Adam that Wendy from the coroner's office called and she went on to explain how the Chases were killed. "Adam, they were butchered alive!"

"Holy mother of God, I can't believe that happened." Adam continued. "Rebecca, please be careful, I love you." Adam just realized what he had said. He said the 'L' word to Rebecca after just one date. Adam thought that Rebecca would think he's pussy whipped.

After he said 'I love you' to Rebecca, an awkward silence occurred. "Thank you Adam, I really appreciate you looking out for me." Rebecca did love Adam, but didn't want to move that quick. Rebecca felt like she had to return the message to Adam. "I love you too Adam." There she said it and she couldn't take it back.

Adam felt relieved that she felt the same way as he did. "I can't wait for you to return home so that we can go on another date."

Rebecca liked hearing that, she loved being with Adam. She knew she liked him the first time she laid eyes on him. "I can't wait to be in your arms again."

Rebecca and Adam said their good-byes and she went to bed. Rebecca needed to get up early to be at the Library of Congress right when they opened their door. The library is a tourist trap in D.C. and getting there early she'll beat the crowd. Rebecca set her alarm for 6am since the library opens at 8:30am. Rebecca went to sleep easily since she knew Adam was alright.

The next morning Rebecca woke up, showered, had breakfast, and went to the Library. A sweet old lady was at the information booth. "Excuse me, I'm with the F.B.I. and I need to research some year books from Lynn Classical High. Could anyone help me locate them? I need the books dated 2010 through 2020."

The old lady looked up at Rebecca. "Of course my dear, could you please fill out this temporary card?" Rebecca filled out the card and handed it back to the librarian. "Perfect, I'll find someone to help you. You may sit at that table over there."

"Thank you so much ma'am." Rebecca walked over to the table that the woman pointed out. She sat there waiting patiently for someone to arrive. Rebecca marveled at the architecture of the library. It was insanely huge with books from floor to ceiling. Every book in America may be placed in the library. She loved the fact that she was sitting in a building that held rare first edition books and millions of other books.

After about an hour went by, Rebecca noticed the old lady coming towards her with a cart filled with yearbooks. "Did you get these books by yourself?"

The old lady started to pile the books on the table. "Yes dear, it's my job to help our customers." Rebecca noticed that she had a lot more books than just 10 years.

"How many years did you go back?" Rebecca asked as she help her pile the books on the table.

"I retrieved 30 years for you dear. Isn't that what you asked for, dear?"

Rebecca didn't want to hurt the old lady's feelings. "Yes, thank you for retrieving these for me, I really appreciate it." The old lady smile at her as she placed the last book on the table.

"Hope you find what you're looking for dear." The old lady took the cart and walked away. Rebecca watched as she disappeared behind a door that read 'employees only'.

Lynn Classical was a very diverse, and Rebecca knew her assailant would be a Caucasian male, so she was able to skip anyone who was African American, Hispanic, or Asian descent. She had to go through at least 10 years of yearbooks. She lifted up the first yearbook, it was from 2020. She flipped through the pages and started to write down names of all the guys that fit her profile. It wasn't going to be an easy task to run all the names she was writing down. She wished that she was able to just bring the books to her office in Fort Lauderdale. "This is going to take me days to go through all these books." Not only was Rebecca writing down all the names, she was at the copy station taking copies of the pictures of who may fit the profile. It was going to be a difficult task, but she was not going to let all this get in the way of finding the killer.

Rebecca felt her phone vibrate and glanced at the text message to see who it was from. The text had no named just a phone number. "Who could be sending me a text?" She opened the phone and read the text.

Good afternoon Rebecca,

Hope you are having fun in Washington. I've been watching you from afar. You're doing a great job investigating all the murders I have committed. I just wanted to let you know that I'm on my way to another friend of yours to pay them a visit. Good luck in finding me.

Love always,

Dr. Peter Monteiro

Rebecca was freaking out. She didn't know anyone except for Adam. She immediately called Adam to warn him about the killer being on his way to kill him. Adam's phone just kept ringing, but he didn't pick up. "Come on Adam; pick up the god damn phone!"

The call went directly into voice mail. "Adam, its Rebecca call me please, its important."

Rebecca hung up the phone and dialed the mysterious phone number that texted her. The phone rang only once as a robotic voice mail answered. Rebecca listened to the message.

"The number you are trying to reach is no longer in service. Please check the number and dial again."

"Fuck the phone must be a temporary throw away phone." Rebecca hung up and called Adam again, this time he picked up.

"Hi Rebecca, sorry I didn't answer your call. I was talking to Mr. Thorton about the case. How's it going in D.C.?"

"Thank God you're alright Adam. I just received a text from Dr. Monteiro. He texted me stating he's going to kill again. You were the only one I can think of that he may hurt. I was so worried about you when you didn't answer your phone."

Adam could hear in her voice that she was truly concerned. "I'm alright Rebecca; nobody is going to hurt me." Adam's voice was hypnotic as Rebecca suddenly calmed down. "So how's it going in Washington? Could you forward the text to me? I can try to find out who sent it, since we know the doctor is dead."

"It's a daunting task making copies of people who fit the profile. I've been at it for hours and haven't had a break. I started with the year 2020 and I'm only on 2017, the year I turned 16. I'm going to call it a day and return tomorrow to finish up."

"That's a great idea Rebecca. Call me as soon as you get to the hotel. I miss you Rebecca and please be safe."

"I'll be safe Adam, I'm carrying my gun." Rebecca laughed and said her goodbyes to Adam. "I'll call you when I get to the hotel." Rebecca hung up the phone and placed it in her purse. She closed the last book she looked at and walked over to the librarian's desk to ask if it would be alright to leave the books on the table and she'll return tomorrow to finish her research.

She waited for almost 20 minutes at the desk and decided to put some of the books away on the cart. Rebecca only needed the year books from 2010 through 2014 to finish off her research. The other 20 years of books could be returned. As Rebecca was placing the books on the cart she heard an unruly noise. She could hear books falling all over the place and then she heard it.

Rebecca then heard a scream from a woman who was in the library. Rebecca ran to where she heard the scream from and found a person underneath a bunch of books. "Don't touch anything!" Rebecca said to the people who started to gather around the accident. "Someone please call 9-1-1!" Rebecca showed her F.B.I. credentials to the onlookers. Rebecca took control of the situation and walked over to the person lying on the floor. "Did anyone see what happened?"

A young woman spoke up. "I saw what happened."

Rebecca looked at the young woman. "Don't go anywhere; I would like to take your statement." Rebecca started to remove the books that were covering the person on the floor. As she carefully removed the books she noticed that it was the sweet old librarian that helped her. She placed her fingers on her neck to feel a pulse and noticed that blood was actually gushing from her neck. Her neck was sliced opened before she fell. Rebecca stood up and saw blood starting to stream towards her feet. She walked away from the victim and talked with the witness. "What did you see?"

The woman with red flaming hair looked like a college kid. "I was doing some research on my history paper that's due tomorrow when I saw something shimmering on the forth level of the library. It looked like a mirror reflecting the sun. The librarian was standing with her back to the railing and I saw a shadow of a man in front of her. He was holding something that was reflecting the sun. Then I saw the man shove her over and she fell to the floor below. I looked up and the guy or woman was gone. It's like they vanished in thin air."

Rebecca looked at the woman. She was visibly shaken by the ordeal. "Thank you for telling me what you had seen. Please wait here until the police shows up and tell them that story."

When the police arrived Rebecca showed them where the victim was and told them that the lady with the red hair witnesses the incident. Rebecca hoped it was just a coincidence that the librarian was killed while she was there at the library.

Rebecca walked over to the table where she was doing her research when she saw one of the investigators walking towards her. "Are you Rebecca Watson?"

"Yes, I'm Rebecca. How may I help you?"

The investigator showed Rebecca his badge. He was a fellow F.B.I. agent just like her. "Miss Watson did you know the victim?"

Rebecca reached into her bag to get her credentials when the agent pulled his gun on her. "Freeze, don't you dare move." He commanded. "Hand me that weapon now and don't do anything crazy or I'll shoot."

Rebecca slowly handed the agent her weapon and he placed it on the floor and kicked it to another agent that heard him yell freeze. He pushed Rebecca over the table knocking over the remainder of the books she hadn't placed on the cart yet. "I'm an F.B.I. agent. Check my credentials." The agent reached into her bag and took out badge and credentials.

The agent removed himself from Rebecca. "I'm sorry Miss Watson, but you didn't identify yourself when I was walking over." The other agent there gave Rebecca her weapon. "I'm agent Nico Dimare."

Rebecca didn't get mad that he almost cuffed her. She knew he was only doing his job. "No need to be sorry Agent Dimare. You were just doing your job." Rebecca stood up and straightened her clothing. "How can I help you Nico?"

Nico and the other agent looked fairly new on the job. Nico was definitely Italian with very dark hair and brown eyes that were almost demon black. His face was scared with acne and his eye brows were connected to look like a dead caterpillar crawled on his forehead. His partner was just standing there letting Nico do all the talking. "Miss Watson we found this on the victim. It's a note addressed to you." Nico handed the evidence bag to Rebecca.

"Do you have any gloves I can use? I would like to see what's in the note."

Nico handed over a pair of gloves so she wouldn't leave any of her fingerprints on the evidence. Rebecca removed the note and opened it slowly.

Dear Miss Watson,

I was so nice seeing you work diligently on the case. You actually got here before I was able to remove what you were looking for in those yearbooks. It was unfortunate that the librarian had to die because of you. Don't you worry though; there will be more deaths on your hands. Hope you burn in hell bitch!

Love always,

Dr. Peter Monteiro

Rebecca folded the note back up and placed it into the evidence bag. She stumbled back in shock that the killer has been watching her all this time while she did her research. As she stumbled she hit the table that she was working on and some of the yearbooks fell to the floor. She bent over to pick them up and one of the books opened to a page that was shocking to her. There was a photo of Willard Thorton. He graduated Lynn Classical back in 2002. Rebecca thought it was strange that all the bio's she read about Mr. Thorton never mentioned he was from Lynn. There wasn't even a mention that he was from Massachusetts. Rebecca tore the page out of the yearbook and started to walk away. "Excuse me, Miss Watson where are you going?"

"I'm going back to my hotel. I'm staying at the Grand Entry on Baltimore Avenue." Rebecca left as fast as she could to get back to her hotel. Her heart was racing and she couldn't believe that she just discovered that her boss, Willard Thorton went to her school in 2002. But before she came to any conclusion she had to investigate further into his youth to see if there was anything that could relate to these killings.

CHAPTER 14

HOMEWARD BOUND

Rebecca went back to her hotel and checked out immediately. She called Adam and told him to meet her in Boston again. Rebecca wanted to tell Adam what she had found but wanted to show him in person. It's never a good thing to accuse your boss of killing several people. Rebecca paid for her airline ticket with her own credit card so Thorton Associates wouldn't know where she was going. She told Adam to do the same and will explain to him why she asked him to pay out of pocket.

Rebecca landed in Boston and her Grandmother picked her up from the airport. Grandma on her father's side was her favorite. She remembered fondly the summers she spent at their house. Rebecca always blamed herself for her grandfather's death, but her grandmother assured her that it wasn't her fault, and it was the evil Sweet Sixteen Killer.

Rebecca entered her grandmother's car and sat there quietly. "Why are you so quiet my dear?" Rebecca didn't want to answer, since she didn't want to worry her, so she just shrugged her shoulders like she didn't know why she was quiet.

When they finally arrived at the apartment where her grandmother was staying, Rebecca thought how sad it was when she decided to sell the house. Rebecca looked around the apartment. "Nice place you have here Grandma."

Rebecca smiled at her and kissed her on the cheek. "Sorry I've been a little distant, but I didn't want to worry you."

"Rebecca, I'm always worried about you. That's what love is all about. Caring for the person you love and praying for their safety." She walked over to Rebecca and gave her a huge hug to comfort her.

"Thank you Grandma, I love you too!" Rebecca smiled at her and kissed her once again on the cheek. "Grandma may I have a talk with you about Gramps?"

"You can talk to me about anything dear. What would you like to know?"

"Well, let's have some coffee and cookies like old times. My co-worker Adam will be here in a few hours and I would like to have that conversation about Gramps with him if you don't mind."

Rebecca's grandmother went into the kitchen to get her some coffee and cookies. Luckily for Rebecca she just finished cooking fresh chocolate chip cookies. There was nothing better than a hot cookie that just came out of the over.

"Here you go dear, coffee with cream and sugar just the way you liked it." Rebecca loved how her grandmother remembered her coffee. "You and your so called co-worker can sleep in the spare room. No need to get a hotel room." She smiled and winked at her.

"Grams, you're embarrassing me. Adam and I are just co-workers." Rebecca lied to her grandmother and she knew that she wasn't going to get away with a lie.

"Whatever you say Rebecca. You're not a child anymore and you are old enough to have a sexual relationship with a co-worker."

Rebecca placed her hands in her face. "Grams, I'm not having this conversation with you."

Rebecca and her grandmother both laughed and sat down around the table to talk about old times. She was enjoying multiple cups of coffee and at least 2 dozen cookies while talking. Even though Rebecca just left Boston a month ago, she hadn't really seen her favorite Grandmother for months. It seems the only time she sees her is on holidays and birthdays. Rebecca received a text from Adam letting her know he'll be there in about 5 minutes. "He's almost here Grams; promise me you won't embarrass me."

"I promise dear, I won't embarrass you much." She laughed and walked into the kitchen. "How does he like his coffee?"

"He likes his coffee like I take it."

Rebecca's grandmother started to brew a new pot of coffee when there was a knock at the door. "That's weird; I usually have to buzz them in the building."

"Don't answer the door Grams. I'll see who's behind the door." Rebecca got up and walked over to the door. There was a young boy around 16 years of age holding a huge bouquet of roses.

"Miss Rebecca Watson, flower delivery for you."

Rebecca opened the door and let the boy in. "Flowers for me, I wonder who sent them?"

"Sorry lady, I don't know who sent them, I just deliver them." Rebecca took the flowers out of the boy's hand and walked over to get some money out of her purse to tip him. "Thank you young man, here's a ten dollar tip."

"Wow, thank you miss!" The boy smiled and shoved the money into his pocket before Rebecca could ask for change. Rebecca closed the door and read the card.

To the only woman in the world who makes me tingle.

The card was only signed with a heart. "Wow, nice to know he's only your co-worker." Rebecca's grandmother said sarcastically.

"You promised Grams not to embarrass me."

Rebecca went to place the roses in a vase with water to keep them fresh. The apartment buzzer rang notifying them that someone was down in the lobby. Rebecca's grandmother walked over to the intercom to answer the buzzer. "Who is it?"

Adam cleared his throat since he was nervous to meet Rebecca's grandmother. "Hi, it's Adam May, I work with your granddaughter Rebecca."

"Ok dear, I'll buzz you in." Rebecca's grandmother pressed the button to let Adam into the apartment complex. She lived on the second floor so he was at her apartment in no time at all. When Adam reached the apartment he knocked on the door. Rebecca's grandmother yell to let Adam know the door was open.

Adam was greeted by Rebecca and escorted him into the kitchen. "Adam, this is Grams; she's the grandmother I actually liked."

Adam walked over to shake Grams hand. "Don't be silly Adam; give your grams a hug." Rebecca put her hands over face. "I can't believe you already broke your promise!" Rebecca's grandmother and Adam both laughed.

"It's a pleasure meeting you Donna."

Rebecca's grandmother slapped Adam across the head. "Call me Grams, your family."

"Adam, here's a cup of coffee, please have a seat." Rebecca placed the cup in front of Adam and they all took a seat.

"So Rebecca, why did I travel all the way to Boston on my own dime? And don't tell me it was because you wanted to introduce me to your grandmother." Adam took a sip of his coffee.

Rebecca unfolded the page of the yearbook she ripped for its binder and placed it in front of Adam. "What am I looking at Rebecca?"

Rebecca sighed and pointed to the picture of a young Willard Thorton. "It's Willard, our boss! He went to my high school and graduated in 2002. Don't you find it weird that in every bio I had ever read about Mr. Thorton, there was nothing listed where he grew up or what high school he attended?"

"That is strange. It says here he was the president of the honor's club and he wanted to open up a multi-billion dollar business. Looks like he accomplished everything he set out to do. Do you think Mr. Thorton has something to do with the killings?"

"I'm not sure Adam, but it's worth looking into. Grams, how much do you know about Dr. Peter Monteiro?"

Rebecca's grandmother sat down around the table with Adam and her. "Well I know it consumed a lot of your grandfather's time. All he ever wanted to do was to solve his brother's murder. That's why he became a cop in the first place." Rebecca's grandmother told the whole story. "As you know dear, your great Uncle Scott was killed September 17th, 1981 on his 16th birthday. Your grandfather never got over his death. Right after high school he joined the police academy and started to snoop around. He was called to a gruesome scene in Lynn Woods where a body was discovered. It was on your great grandmother's birthday, May 30th, 2014. He told me it was a 16 year old boy and it reminded him of a case he worked on back on the same date in 2000." Rebecca's grandmother took a sip of her coffee. She seemed to be upset about telling the story.

"Would you like to stop Grams?" Rebecca asked her grandmother.

"No, I'm alright dear, I'll continue with the story." She took another sip of her coffee. "Back in 2000, your grandfather was only an officer and not a detective yet. He was the first to arrive at the scene. A young girl was found on an empty lot with her next sliced open. Your grandfather started to see a pattern. She and the boy in Lynn Woods both turned 16 that day, just like your great uncle. All were killed on their 16th birthday."

"And then what happened Grams?" Rebecca asked.

"Well your grandfather started to dig deeper. He realized that there have been at least 34 kids killed on their 16th birthday. I mean, you could just imagine how the kid felt when he found the girl lying in the field killed. I mean other people found the dead bodies too, but they were much older."

"You mean a kid found one of the victims. Do you remember his name?" Adam asked.

Rebecca's grandmother rose from her chair and disappeared into her bedroom. Within a few minutes, she carried out a huge box filled with files. "Let me help you with that box Grams." Adam took the box from her arms and placed it on the table.

"The file should be in here somewhere." Grams started to shuffle through the files. "Here it is, Sally Latimer, found on an empty lot on Western Ave." Grams opened the file and started to read through it. "He interviewed a young African American that lived on Western Ave; his name was Willard Thorton, 16 he lived at 182 Western Avenue."

Rebecca and Adam just looked at each other in shock. They just realized that Mr. Thorton found a body left by Dr. Monteiro. "Holy mother God, this can't be true Adam! Does this make our boss the prime suspect?"

Adam picked up the folder and read the report written by the detective. "Well, let's not get ahead of ourselves. Mr. Thorton is a very secretive man. I'm sure there's a reason why his bio doesn't include where he lived as a child."

Rebecca took another file out of the box and examined it. "Well, the lab did a DNA test and it came back as Dr. Monteiro. What if they made a mistake? What if, and this is just a hypothetical question, Mr. Thorton is somehow related to Dr. Monteiro?"

"That's a good theory; however we would have to get DNA from Mr. Thorton. How will we go about getting his DNA to test it?"

"I'm not sure, but I'm positive we'll be able to think of a plan to retrieve his DNA." Rebecca and Adam both started to shift around the files to see if there were any other links between Mr. Thorton and Dr. Monteiro. Rebecca's grandmother supplied them with plenty of coffee as they both worked until 2am. "Adam, look at the time. We've been at this for hours and haven't found any other link to Dr. Monteiro. I'm going to call some of my pals at the F.B.I. and asked them if they can retrieve Mr. Thorton's birth certificate."

Adam yawned and stood up and stretched his arms. "That sounds like a great idea, Rebecca. Let's get some sleep and start up tomorrow morning. Maybe there are people still living in the area that might have remembered Mr. Thorton." Adam extended his hand so he could lead Rebecca to the bed room. "I know you're exhausted from traveling and looking through 30 plus years of files."

Adam was right, Rebecca was exhausted and she needed to go to sleep. "You're right, let's go to sleep and we'll work on this tomorrow."

Adam held her hand and led her into the bedroom. He closed the door and whispered softly into Rebecca's ear. "How sound proof are the walls?"

Rebecca smiled and knew exactly what he meant. "Let's find out."

CHAPTER 15

MAY 30TH, 2000

It was just another normal day for Willard. He was out of school and had to work at George's Grocery Store. Willard, only being 16, was way ahead of boys his own age. Willard was a straight 'A' student and loved to be active in school by joining as many clubs that he could handle. Willard attended Lynn Classical High and was well on his way to be the valedictorian.

Willard worked that day from opening to 9am. Willard was usually in school that Tuesday morning, but it was closed for a teacher's meeting. Willard just thought that since Monday was the Memorial Day holiday, the teachers just wanted to extend their 3 days off to 4. Willard didn't mind getting up at the crack of dawn to help his boss George. George loved that Willard was always dependable and he could always count on him when needed.

Willard started to walk home from George's at 9am. He always took the same path home and always jumped the fence into a deserted lot on Western Avenue. The lot was covered with weeds higher than an elephant's eye. It wasn't a huge lot, just big enough for a short cut to his house.

As he was walking through the tall brush, something shinny caught his eye and he wanted to investigate. He was getting closer to the object and he noticed that it was a gold bracelet. Willard knelt down to pick it up, and as he was getting up, he noticed the girl who wasn't moving. Willard walked over to the girl to see if she needed help. When he reached her he noticed that it was too late, the girl was dead. Her throat was slashed and he knew by the amount of blood around her she wasn't alive. "Holy mother fucker!" Willard shouted as he saw the girl.

The girl was about the same age as Willard and she was white as a puffy cloud. She looked familiar to him and thought she might have gone to his school. Willard needed to go get help even though he knew there was no help for her. Willard stood up and looked at the girl one more time before he ran to the street.

Willard started to wave his arms around for someone to stop to call the cops. A gentleman finally stopped his Jaguar to see what Willard wanted. "Are you alright, boy?" The stranger was dressed to the T. The suit he wore was made with the finest silk and the car he drove was a top of the line Jaguar.

"Sir, can I borrow your phone? I need to call the police right away." Willard was out of breath from running to the street even though it wasn't that far, it was probably due to nerves.

"What's going on?" The stranger got out of his car and walked up to Willard.

"There's a dead girl just lying there in the weeds." Willard told the man.

"Well young man, why don't you show me?" The man seemed a little bit skeptical.

Willard started to walk towards the woman and pointed to where she laid. "She's right over there! I know she's dead, her throat is slashed open."

The man walked over and looked at the dead girl. He seemed to be staring at her for the longest time. "Dude, are you going to call for help or not?"

The man turned towards Willard and took out his cell phone and dialed 9-1-1.

"9-1-1 what's your emergency?"

"Hi, I'm standing on an emptied lot on Western Avenue." The man paused. "Hey kid, what's the address here?"

"325 Western Avenue, sir." Willard responded.

"Just send a cruiser to 325 Western Avenue, a young man had just discovered a young woman dead in the field."

"What is your name sir?" The operator needed the information.

"That's not important, just send a damn cruiser!" The man yelled at the woman on the phone and hung up. "Well kid, you better stick around. The cops will want to ask you some questions."

The man started to walk away from Willard. "Where are you going? Aren't you going to be here when the cops show up?"

"Not my problem kid, you found her, you stay here." The man heard the sirens from a cruiser approaching and jumped in his car and drove away.

Willard didn't know what to do. Should he wait or leave? He was thinking to himself that the cops are going to blame him and arrest him for murder. They always blame the black kid Willard thought to himself.

The police cruiser pulled up to the emptied lot and noticed Willard standing alone at the edge of the lot. The cop was tall, much taller than Willard. He had short blond hair that was styled like a military soldier. To Willard the cop look like a mountain. The cop walked over to Willard and told him his name. Willard was still in shock and the cops name went in one ear and out the other.

"Can you show me what you found?" The cop asked.

Willard pointed in the field towards the chain link fence. The cop walked through waist deep weeds to get to the scene. There he noticed the young girl with blond hair. She was fully clothed in a pretty red dress. Her shoes were missing and her neck was slashed. The cop took his radio out and confirmed the situation.

The cop started to walk towards Willard and stopped directly in front of him. "So, how did you find the body?

Willard answered the cop's question. "Well, I was walking through the field and I found her like that."

"So why were you walking through an empty weeded field?"

"I live right there, in the gray house. 182 Western Avenue."

The cop turned around and saw where Willard lived. The house was gray and run down and he could see the paint peeling off the side of the building. The cop started to bombard Willard with questions. "What's your name? What's your phone number? Where were you coming from? Did you know the girl?"

Willard lifted his arms since he was getting confused with all the questions being thrown at him. "Wow man, one question at a time!" Willard snapped at the cop. "My name is Willard Thorton and my phone number is 555-2536. I was coming home from work. I work at Georges Grocery Store. I've never see this girl before, and I don't know where or how she got here or how she got killed." Willard began to get nervous. He felt like he was being interrogated. "I swear man, ask my boss. I was there all morning."

The cop looked Willard up and down to see if he was lying to him. "No kid, you're not in any trouble, but stay around in case the detectives want to talk with you. OK?"

Willard shook his head in agreement that he would stick around. The cop walked over to the detective on the scene. Willard saw that the cop was telling the detective everything he just said and pointed towards Willard. One of the detectives walked over to Willard. "Hi Willard, my name is Detective Vlahos. I'll be working on the case. Is there anything else you remember that you weren't able to discuss with the officer?"

"No sir, I told him everything I know." Willard seemed more comfortable talking with the detective than the cop. "May I leave now sir?"

"Sure kid, I got your number if I need to talk with you again."

Willard started to walk home and the guy in the Jaguar pulled over. "Thanks for leaving me high and dry over there!"

"Sorry kid, I had to leave. I'm not comfortable around cops." The guy said.

"So you leave a black kid standing there near a dead white girl. Are you fucking crazy man? Really, any white girl that shows up dead, the first thing the cops look for is a black man." Willard started to walk away from the car.

The guy drove his car slowly to keep in stride with Willard walking. "Get in the car kid."

"Sorry dude, I'm not a trick and I don't do guys for money." Willard almost had enough of this guy.

"Tell me, did you enjoy seeing that girl dead? Did you like the blood? Did you see how nice that neck was slashed? Don't be shy boy; we all have our dark side. I just wanted to know how you felt."

"Who the fuck are you man?" Willard thought this guy was crazy. "Leave me the fuck alone or I'll yell so loud that the cops will arrest your honky white ass." Willard never used harsh language, and rarely ever used racist slurs.

"Willard, get in the car." The guy demanded. "We need to talk. You can talk to me. I'm a doctor. Dr. Peter Monteiro."

Willard stopped and looked into the guy's car. "How do you know my name? And what kind of doctor are you?"

"I'm a psychologist, and I'll explain everything. Just get into the car." Dr. Monteiro unlocked the door and Willard got in.

"So, what do you have to tell me?" Willard asked.

CHAPTER 16

DNA DINNER

Rebecca and Adam flew back to Fort Lauderdale to figure out a plan to recover some of Mr. Thorton's DNA. Rebecca called the F.B.I headquarters in Washington D.C. to see if they would be able to obtain the birth certificate of Willard Thorton. That request was going to be hard since all of Willards bio's had no date of birth or the actually city he was born in. Rebecca knew that if he was born in Lynn, then most likely his birth certificate burnt with the City Hall burning down. With the schools burning down and city hall, it all pointed to suspect Willard is somehow behind all these murders. He also knew every step Rebecca took. He knew every suspect or witnesses that Adam and she talked with. The longer Rebecca thought about it, the more he fit the profile. She was kind of dumbfounded that she was looking for a white male in his late 20's to early 30's. "How could I be so stupid?" Rebecca said out loud.

"What did you say Rebecca?" Adam asked knowing damn well what she just said.

"How can I be so stupid Adam? My profile that I gave the Fort Lauderdale police was all wrong! I'm never wrong. Yet, if Mr. Thorton is responsible for all these killings, then there goes my theory of a white male in his 20's or 30's."

"We all make mistakes Rebecca; I wouldn't dwell on it right now. We have to figure a way to get Mr. Thorton's DNA." Adam paused for a moment. "I have a great idea!"

"What's the idea Adam?"

"What if we invite Mr. Thorton to dinner? We could say that we would like to run a few things by him as we continue to investigate the case. During dinner we can get his napkin or something he used with his mouth."

"That's a brilliant idea Adam!"

"See, that's why you keep me around, I'm brilliant." Adam laughed and so did Rebecca.

"Sure that's the reason, or could it be your great in bed?" Rebecca winked at Adam.

Adam was hot in bed. He knew how to please a woman and knew all the sensual pleasure spots that make a woman squirm. Rebecca couldn't get enough of him. She loved everything about him, from his smile, from the way he smells. He just turned Rebecca on.

Adam pulled up to Rebecca's condo. "Would you like to come up Adam?"

Adam smiled at Rebecca. "I would love to, but I really need some rest. Remember, we didn't sleep last night and we just arrived home after 3 hour flight."

Rebecca understood what Adam was saying. Even a super hero needs their rest. "Alright Adam, I totally understand. When do you plan to ask Mr. Thorton to dinner?"

"I'll call you later today with the details. That's if Mr. Thorton accepts our invitation to have dinner with us."

"Sounds like a plan Adam, I look forward to your call."

Rebecca closed the car door and started to walk towards the entrance to the building where she lived at. Adam love to watch Rebecca, she had the nicest ass Adam has ever seen. "Damn she's hot!"

Adam drove off before he changed his mind about going in with her. He had to think with his brain and not his dick. Adam arrived at his apartment and opened the door. His apartment was dark and he turned on the lights on. Adam couldn't believe his eyes. His entire apartment was ransacked. Chairs flipped over, his couch torn apart, the stuffing from the sofa was everywhere.

His glass table was shattered to pieces. He walked around looking at the mess and then he saw it. A dead chicken with his head cut off. The trail of the chicken's blood led him to his bedroom, and when he walked in there was writing on the wall. Written in chicken blood it read 'stop looking, or you'll be next'. Adam sat on his bed and took a picture of the wall with his cell phone. He attached the picture to a text he sent to Rebecca.

Rebecca, I just arrived at home to ransacked apartment. The photo of the blood written message was on my bedroom wall. I really think that Mr. Thorton is behind these acts of violence. You have me convinced that it's him. We definitely need his DNA as soon as possible. Would it be possible to stay with you until I get this mess cleaned up? Please let me know. Love you!

Rebecca felt her phone vibrate and read Adam's message. She immediately called him. Adam answered the phone with it ringing just once. "Adam, get your fucking ass over here now. You didn't have to ask me to stay at my place; you know that you're more than welcome to stay any time!"

"Thanks Rebecca, I just feel safer with someone who owns a gun. I'll be there within the hour. Let me gather some clothes and I'll be there as soon as possible."

"Ok, just get here quickly. I don't want you to be the next person I know that gets killed. I'll talk with you when you get here." Rebecca hung up her phone and sat on her bed. She was worried that Adam would be the next one to be killed. Her feelings for him were strong. Even though Rebecca was a strong woman that can handle carnage, she never been in a serious relationship with anyone. She knew she was falling in love with Adam and she would do anything to protect him. She melted when she read the words 'love you' in Adam's text message. But she also wondered if it was just a friendly gesture or did he actually have feelings for her.

Adam arrived at Rebecca's condo within the hour. When he walked through the door Rebecca ran up to him and threw herself into his arms. "Thank God you're alright Adam." Rebecca hugged him and didn't want to let go. The cologne he was wearing was intoxicating. "We have to convince Mr. Thorton to come to dinner and he can't say no. We'll tell him it's urgent."

"We need to come up with a story first Rebecca. Have you thought of anything?"

Adam and Rebecca sat on the sofa trying to think of something so that Mr. Thorton would attend dinner with them. "I think our best course of action is to ask him for some advice and ask him what his profile would be." Adam suggested a plan that Rebecca really didn't care for.

"Adam, what makes you think that he'll show up? I mean, he just might say 'we can talk at work about it." Rebecca made sense, and Mr. Thorton would be too smart to fall for something like that. "How about we just invite him to dinner so I can thank him personally for giving me the job?"

"Ok, we'll go with your plan, but I don't think he'll accept the invitation." Adam picked up his work cell and called Mr. Thorton. "Hello, Mr. Thorton, its Adam. Rebecca and I would like to extend an invitation for dinner. Rebecca would like to thank you for the opportunity you have given her. Would you please meet us at Bistro Mezzaluna around 8pm tonight?" Adam waited for Mr. Thorton to answer. "No problem Mr. Thorton, I'll tell Rebecca." Adam hung up the phone and turned to Rebecca.

"Well? What did he say?"

"He said he'll go on one stipulation."

"And what's that?"

"He'll only go if he can pay for dinner. He's stubborn like that and loves to pay. Looks like the mouse took the bait and he's even paying us to do it."

Rebecca's phone started to ring and she noticed it was from the F.B.I. "Rebecca speaking, how can I help you?" Rebecca was listening to the person on the other end for about 10 minutes. She was writing down everything the person on the other end was telling her. She hung up and turned to Adam. "Well that was the F.B.I headquarters. They ran Mr. Thorton's background for me. He was born October 31st, 1984 in Saugus Hospital to a Helen Thorton. There is no mention of a father on Mr. Thorton's birth certificate. They also did some digging on Helen Thorton. She was just 18 years old when she gave birth to her son Willard. She was born in Lynn Hospital November 1st, 1966. Helen lived with her parents until Willard was 3. She moved out to a luxury apartment, though she had no job. They're not sure who was paying for her apartment. When Willard turned 16 he went to live with his aunt on Western Ave right down the street where he found the girl in the empty lot. According to her record, Helen was arrested and charged with prostitution and found guilty when he was 16. She went to prison and died of an overdose while incarcerated. Willard was orphaned yet still excelled in High School where he graduated Valedictorian and went to Harvard University on a full scholarship. He then graduated with honors and became one of the best defense lawyers in the country." Rebecca paused to take a breather. "The rest you'll be able to read in his bio." Rebecca was becoming angry. "Adam, I know this son of a bitch is guilty, but he's squeaky clean. What is the connection between Dr. Monteiro and Mr. Thorton?"

Adam held Rebecca in his arms tight. "Hopefully something will show up in his DNA."

Rebecca and Adam both got ready for dinner. "You look amazing in that dress. Blue is definitely your color."

"Thank you Adam, you look sharp tonight too." Rebecca walked over to Adam and gave him a long passionate kiss.

Adam had to push Rebecca away. "We better stop or our clothes will be on the floor."

Rebecca smile at Adam and agreed they had to stop kissing. "I hope we don't accidently kiss in front of Mr. Thorton tonight. I'm not sure what the policy is on dating co-workers."

"I think the policy is don't ask, don't tell. Don't you just love being in the service again?" Adam laughed.

The two of them headed for Bistro Mezzaluna and arrived on time. When they walked into the restaurant they noticed that Mr. Thorton was already seated. Rebecca extended her hand. "Thank you for coming Mr. Thorton."

"Please Rebecca, call me Willard."

The three of them sat at the table and was having a great time and conversation. "I'd like to make a toast." Willard raised his glass of wine. "To Rebecca, the newest member of our team, thank you for coming to Thorton Associates, and thank you for making Adam happy." Willard winked at Rebecca.

Rebecca almost choked on her wine. "You know about Adam and me?"

Willard laughed out loud. "How can you not notice the chemistry between you two? Rebecca, you're glowing and I never seen Adam smile so much. I know you two just met, but if you're afraid of what I think or will do to you,

you got me all wrong. I'm not against office romance, and I definitely don't get in the way of love."

Willard placed his napkin on top of his plate after he wiped his mouth. "Will you two excuse me? I need to head to the restroom." Willard stood up and proceeded to go to the restroom.

Rebecca looked at Adam and removed Willard's napkin and placed it in her purse. The called the waiter over to remove their plates and napkins so Mr. Thorton wouldn't realize his was missing. The waiter cleared the table and brought over new napkins and spoons for the dessert they had ordered. Willard walked back to the table and notice everything was cleaned up. "This is why I love this place; they clean up between each meal."

After dinner was over, Adam and Rebecca said their goodbyes. "Willard, thank you so much for dinner. I'm so happy I joined your team of profilers and I'm looking forward to meeting the rest of the crew when they return from their assignments."

Rebecca leaned in and hugged Willard. "Your welcome Rebecca, and like I said, I'm so glad you two are there for each other especially since there's a maniac trying to kill you and anyone who is close to you." Willard got into his brand new Bentley and drove away.

"We got to go to the police crime lab to get this napkin tested." Rebecca said to Adam.

"You're right, let's go!"

The two of them arrived at the Ft. Lauderdale police station and went directly to the crime lab. An older gentleman in a long white lab coat was sitting at the desk within the lab. "Excuse me; I'm Rebecca Watson from the F.B.I. I need this napkin analyzed as soon as possible. I need D.N.A. ran on the napkin and I need the results like yesterday!"

The crime lab associate took the napkin and swabbed it for a D.N.A. sample. "This will take at least an hour to run. Would you like to wait around?"

Adam and Rebecca both answered at the same time. "Yes!"

The two of them paced the floor for over an hour. Rebecca looked at her cell phone for the time. "Jesus, it's been way over an hour! I were in Washington, I'd have the information within 20 minutes."

"Relax Rebecca; we'll have an answer soon." Adam took Rebecca into his arms and squeezed her tightly.

The lab technician walked into the room holding a piece of paper. "I have your results. According to the national data base, the D.N.A. sample you gave me is a 99.9% match. Who's ever D.N.A. you retrieved is definitely the son of Dr. Peter Monteiro, renowned serial killer."

Rebecca and Adam looked at each other in amazement. "That fucking son of a bitch is the Sweet Sixteen Killer's son! I knew it was him all along. Adam, what are we going to do?"

"We'll figure something out Rebecca." Adam comforted Rebecca.

CHAPTER 17

DADDY DEAREST

Willard and Dr. Monteiro drove away in his Jaguar. "I'm not sure how to say this to you Willard, but I'm your father."

Willard looked at Peter. "My mom told me you were wealthy, but she never told me who you were. Where were you when she died man?"

Peter slowed his car down and pulled into an empty parking lot. "Helen, your mom, didn't want me around. She was young and I was still in college becoming a doctor. I supported you and your mother for years, until your mom lost her way. Your old enough, and intelligent enough to understand what I'm about to tell you."

Willard looks down and a tear rolled down his cheek. "My mom died because of you! Why weren't you there to help her with her addiction?"

Willard started to open the car door, but it was locked and had the safety locks on. "Calm down Willard, let's go to my house." Peter left the empty parking lot and drove to his house. They pulled into a long driveway and Willard admired how his house was situated on the beach. The home was beautifully landscaped and the old Victorian style home was in mint condition. Peter got out of the car and opened the door for Willard. Willard thought of running from him, but he was curious in what Peter had to say.

The two of them walked into Peter's home and Willard couldn't believe his eyes. The inside of the house was immaculate and designed with a modern interior that did not match the Victorian style outside. The kitchen was huge with a center island that cascaded with expensive Italian marble. The floors were hard oak and buffed so shiny you could see your reflection. The living room was decorated with contemporary furniture and he had a television projector that projected on a hidden screen. Willard walked around in amazement. "Take a seat Willard, we need to talk."

Willard sat down on the leather sofa. "Ok old man, speak."

Peter walked over to his closet and took out some photo albums. "I always said when you turned 16 I would talk to you. Your mother and I were in love, but our families didn't approve of a biracial couple. Back then, things were more difficult for a white man and a black woman to be involved with each other. It's accepted now, but not then. It's like being gay in the 70's and 80's; nobody was out of the closet. Now everyone is out. Shit, even the high schools have gay, straight alliance." Peter handed one of the photo albums to Willard.

Willard opened the photo album and began looking at pictures of a younger version of Peter. "How old were you in this picture?"

Peter glanced at the picture. "That was taken on the worse day of my life. It was on my sixteenth birthday."

Willard scratched his head. "Really, why was turning 16 the worse day of your life?"

Peter took a deep breath. "Well that's the day my mom died of a heart attack preparing my birthday dinner. I found her on the kitchen floor when I got home from school. My dad beat the living shit out of me that day and blamed me for her death."

"Wow man, that sucks!"

"I vowed that I wouldn't let anyone who turned sixteen be devastated like I was. My father beat me every day. The final straw is when I was sleeping; he came into my room and raped me. That's the night I ran from my home and never looked back." Peter continued with his story. "I left that son of a bitch a letter telling him if he ever tried to find me I would have him arrested for raping a young boy."

"Oh my God man, that's terrible. Did he ever try to look for you?"

"No, that night after reading my letter. He went into the den with a double barrel shot gun and blew his own head off. The asshole couldn't bear to live knowing I could someday ruin his life. That was the best day of my life. Even though I was orphaned I was ready to live my life. So at 16 I left my town in Nevada and came to Boston where I excelled as a student. I was the youngest intern at Beth Israel Hospital."

Willard looked amazed and excited hearing Peter's stories. "So why did you choose Psychology?"

"Well, I wanted to help those in need mentally. I work with teens and pre-teens. A lot of my patients are from broken homes and are trying to deal with divorce. Some of my patients are struggling with their sexuality. My specialty is hypnosis."

"Really, you can hypnotize someone? Could you do it to me? I've never been hypnotized."

Peter started to laugh. "I'm sure I'll be hypnotizing you soon. But you still need to know exactly who I am Willard. I need to ask you a few questions. Is that alright with you?"

Willard shrugged his shoulders. "Sure, ask me anything."

"I know all about your life. What school you go to and what grades you are making. You're well on your way to becoming valedictorian. I guess my genes of intelligence were passed down to you. I also know that you work for George's Groceries and you're currently dating Jill Cannon, who is only 15."

"You're scaring me man. How do you know so much about me?"

"Just because I wasn't in your life, doesn't mean I wasn't in your life. I've watched you grow into a young man, 16 years old and is already about to graduate with honors. You are a remarkable young man."

"Well if you know so much about me, then what else do you need to know?" Willard couldn't believe that Peter knew him inside and out. He kept flipping through pages after pages of photos that were taken from a distant. Pictures of Willard playing little league baseball. Peter had pictures of his 1st birthday party, his first day of school, and at his mother's funeral. "Wait a minute; you were at my mom's funeral?"

Peter nodded yes to Willard. "I was at every important mile stone in your life Willard." Peter paused and stood up and walked to the kitchen. "Would you like a soda?"

"Yes please, that would be great."

Peter grabbed a couple of sodas out of the fridge and walked back to the sofa. Willard put down the photo albums and took a sip of his soda.

"So Willard, what was going on in your head when you found that poor girl in the lot?"

"Are you trying to analyze me?"

"Maybe, but think of it as a free session. And whatever is said here stays within these walls" Peter paused just for a second. "Are you able to keep secretes too?"

"Yes, I'm not a snitch. I keep a lot of secretes."

"That's good to hear Willard. So tell me what you really thought when you found that girl."

Willard took another sip of his soda and took a deep breath. "Well at first I was afraid, then I curious. I wondered who the fuck would do something like this. I mean the girl was about my age, she was beautiful."

"Did you touch her?"

Willard gave Peter a dirty look. "I mean, did you check her pulse?"

"No, I didn't want to get my hands bloody."

"Would you like to see my hobby Willard?"

"Sure, what is it?"

Peter stood up and walked to the closet and grabbed another photo album. "Here, look through that photo album and you'll see what I like to do as a hobby."

"What is it, a stamp collection?" Willard slowly opened the album. His eyes were shocked to see pictures of the young girl in the field. The photos were taken from different angles. "What the fuck is this man?" Willard screamed as he stood up. "I'm getting the fuck out of here!"

Peter stood up and with a stern voice yelled back at him. "Stop right there young man!" Willard stopped in his tracks. "Sit your fucking ass down! I'm not finished with you!"

Willard walked back to the sofa shaking like a leaf in a wind storm. "Please don't hurt me!" Willard begged.

"I'm not going to hurt you. I may not have been your dad, but I am your father. Why on earth would I hurt my own son? Now sit down and look at the photos in that book and tell me what you think."

Willard began to see other photos of young men and women. All of them with their throats slashed open. Willard looked up at Peter and saw that he was enjoying sharing his photos with him. "Did you kill all these people?"

Peter placed his hand on Willard's lap. "I wouldn't say kill, more like put them out of their misery. You see Willard, like I told you what happened to me on my 16th birthday, I don't want any of that to happen to them."

"So you killed them all on their birthday? That's fucked up man!" Willard removed his hand from his lap. "Did you want to kill me on my birthday?"

"I can't lie to you Willard, I'm not a liar, but yes, I wanted to slice your sweet little neck open and watch the blood drain from your body. However, you were with family the entire fucking day celebrating your 16th birthday." Willard tries to leave the sofa again. Peter grabbed his wrist. "Hold on, let me explain."

"Explain? What the fuck do you have to explain? You just said you were going to kill me!"

"Willard, relax and take a deep breath." Peter was an expert in hypnotizing people. "That's good Willard, breathe slowly and deeply." Willard's eyes were getting heavier and heavier. "Listen to the sound of my voice Willard. My voice is soothing and pleasant. You'll hear every word I say, but will not respond. You're in a deep sleep." Willard's head fell forward as he fell asleep.

Peter took all the albums and placed them back in the closet. He sat next to Willard. "You will remember nothing from the time you walked into my home. You never saw any photos. You don't know I'm a killer. I'm just the father you never knew and just met. We are just sitting here trying to get to know each other. When you awake, you'll feel refreshed. You'll be tired and will ask me to take you home. When I count to 3, you'll open your eyes. 1, 2, 3, open your eyes."

Peter stood up with Willard. "Sure, I'd love to take you out for dinner to get to know my son. Are you available Friday night?"

"Friday night is perfect. I have nothing planned." Willard extended his hand. They shook hands and left the house. They arrived at Willards house on Western Ave and a women was standing at the door with her arms crossed. "Shit, that's my aunt! What am I going to say to her?"

"Just tell her what happened in the field and I work for the Lynn police department. You can tell her I'm a counselor that helps with traumatic events. Tell her the police made you talk to me. You'll be alright Willard."

Willard opened the car door and got out. "Thank you Dr. Monteiro." Willard closed the car door.

"You're welcome Willard. I you need to talk, you have my business card." Peter waved goodbye and drove away.

"Who was that guy in the car?" Willard's aunt asked.

"It's a long story Auntie; I'll explain it to you at dinner. I'm starving, what are we having?"

"I cooked your favorite, chicken and dumplings."

The two of them started to walk in the apartment building where Willard lived. Under his breath he whispered. "I know all about you dad. Too bad your hypnosis didn't work on me." A slight grin appeared on his face. A little evilness was revealed. Willard thought to himself 'Will I become my father? I did enjoy seeing that girl. Does it make me a sick man for getting aroused by all those people in that book with their necks slit open?' Willard walked into the apartment and closed the door. "See you Friday night dad!"

CHAPTER 18

THE FINAL CONFRONTATION

Rebecca and Adam left the police station. "Adam, should we inform Detective Swanson?"

Adam turned to Rebecca and held her tight. "Rebecca, you're an F.B.I. agent. We don't need some southern cop to do our business. We can handle this alone. You got this Rebecca. You can do it! Let's take this mother fucker down together. Why let Detective Swanson get all the credit for our work? I've never took anyone down, and I want to know that feeling." Adam kissed Rebecca on the cheek. "I love you Rebecca and I'll be by your side when we take Willard Thorton to jail!"

Rebecca took a deep breath and looked directly into Adam's eyes. "You're right Adam if anyone can do this, I can! Let's go to my place and devise a plan."

The both of them got into Adam's car and drove to Rebecca's condo. Once inside they couldn't control their animal desires and tore each other's clothes off. Adam carried Rebecca to her bed and laid on top of her. He looked directly into her eyes and whispered. "You're an amazing woman Rebecca." They made love for the entire afternoon and were drenched in sweat. They both laid silently on the bed and just looked at the ceiling. "We better get dressed. We have to think of a plan to corner Mr. Thorton."

Rebecca turned to Adam. "What I really want to do is just lay here with you for the rest of my life." Rebecca ran her hand on Adam's chest and started to go lower to his groin.

Adam let out a small moan. "Rebecca, that feels amazing, but you have to stop. We have to work on this case before Mr. Thorton strikes again."

Rebecca knew he was right again, but all she wanted was to be by his side. Adam got out of the bed and walked stark naked to the bathroom. Rebecca admired his physique as he walked. Adam had the nicest butt she ever seen, not to mention he had the biggest cock she ever had in her. Adam had no flaws in Rebecca's eyes. He was perfect in every way. She thought about following him into the bath and maybe take a shower together, but she knew she wouldn't be able to keep her hands off him. "Concentrate on the case Rebecca." She said out loud.

Rebecca got out of bed and threw on a robe. She walked into the kitchen and made herself a coffee. "Adam, would you like a coffee?"

Adam couldn't hear her since his head was under the shower spray. Rebecca poured him a cup of coffee anyway and couldn't remember how he liked his coffee. "Fuck! Does he like it black or with cream and sugar?" She put the cup on the counter and left the cream and sugar next to the cup of coffee.

Holding her coffee, she walked in the bathroom where Adam was drying off. "It's a shame you have to get dressed."

Adam looked up and saw her standing there with a huge smile on her face. "Rebecca are you treating me like a piece of meat?" He laughed.

"Don't be silly, you're more than a piece of meat. You're the entire meal!"

They both laughed as Rebecca took off her robe and stepped into the shower. Like Rebecca, Adam loved every curve on her body. Adam was getting aroused and had to walk out of the bathroom before it was too late. He knew if he stayed there he wouldn't be able to curb his appetite and lust for her.

Adam went into the bedroom and got dressed. As he walks towards the kitchen he noticed the coffee with a little note attached to his mug. "Sorry Adam, don't hate me. I forgot how you liked your coffee. I love you, Rebecca!" Adam took the note and placed it in his shirt pocket. He added cream and 3 sugars to his coffee and sat on the barstool next to the kitchen island and waited for Rebecca to get dressed.

Rebecca walked out of the bedroom with just a t-shirt and jeans on. "Even when you dress like a bum, you're still sexy." Adam grabbed her by the waist and pulled her in for a kiss. "I take my coffee with cream and 3 sugars. Just so you know in the future Mrs. May."

Rebecca was caught off guard when Adam called her Mrs. May. Was he proposing? They only knew each other for a couple of weeks. Were they going too fast? Rebecca pulled away from Adam and sat next to him on the barstool. "So how are we going to catch this bastard?" Just as Rebecca said that she received a text. "Adam, guess who just sent me a text."

"Was it Mr. Thorton?"

"Yes, it says here, emergency! Come to the office now!" Rebecca looked at Adam. "This is a perfect opportunity to corner him."

"Well I'm going with you."

Rebecca looked at Adam and saw a serious look on his face. "I'm going alone Adam. I'm able to take care of myself. Remember, I'm a trained F.B.I. agent and I'm well equipped to handle him."

Adam shook his head in disgust. "Fine, then I'll be waiting for you in the car in front of the office."

Rebecca had no choice but to let him wait in the car. She knew that if she didn't let him go, he wouldn't let her go alone. "That's fine Adam; you can wait in the car. I'll call your cell phone when we arrive, so that you'll be able to hear what's going on when I get in his office, and if you think that I'm in any sort of danger, you can call the police or detective Swanson."

Adam agreed to the plan and the both drove to their work place. When they arrived at Thorton Associates, Rebecca turned to Adam and gave him a kiss on the cheek. "Stop worrying, I'll be fine Adam." Rebecca dialed Adam's cell phone and left the line open so he could hear everything that's going on. "I have my blue tooth device in my ear. You'll be able to hear the entire conversation. Don't be a fucking hero Adam. I don't want anything to happen to you."

Rebecca gave Adam a long passionate kiss before leaving the car. "I love you Adam!" She closed the door and entered the office building. Some of the windows were still blown out from the bomb that was sent to her. She got off the elevator and she could still smell the gun powder that was used in the bomb. She walked towards the door of Mr. Thorton and knocked.

"Come in, it's open." Rebecca opened the door and saw Mr. Thorton sitting at his desk. He looked up from his work and noticed Rebecca. "I'm glad you could make it Rebecca. Please have a seat."

Rebecca walked up to the desk and sat down on the chair that was placed in front. "What's the emergency Mr. Thorton?"

"I know you've only been here a couple of weeks. And within those weeks you were almost killed. Never mind all the people that were killed because of you."

"And what's your point Mr. Thorton?"

"Rebecca, I love having you here, but I need you to be safe." Willard handed Rebecca a couple of airline tickets.

"What's this?" She asked curiously.

"I want you to take Adam to my villa in Italy. Only until they find out who's behind all these killings." Willard looked really concerned but Rebecca wasn't having it.

"Let's cut the shit!" Rebecca raised her voice. "I know dam well who you are!"

Willard was taken off guard. "Excuse me? What are you talking about Rebecca?"

Rebecca stood up from her chair and threw the tickets in his face. "I know you've been killing everyone!" Rebecca continued. "I know you're the son of Dr. Peter Monteiro, also known as the Sweet Sixteen Killer. You've been taking revenge for your dead father."

Willard stood up and confronted Rebecca. "You're right; I am the son of Dr. Monteiro. But I'm no killer Rebecca. In fact, I've been trying to keep you safe. Why do you think I hired you? I don't buy all my employees condos. I did it because I wanted to keep an eye on you and make sure you're safe."

Rebecca gave him an evil laugh. "You really think I'm going to believe that excuse?"

"Rebecca, let me explain. When I found out who my father was at sixteen I was devastated. I didn't want to be related to that monster. Then when your grandfather caught him and he was found not guilty I was shocked as much as everyone else in that town. I read in the paper that he threatened to kill you. I was even more shocked to see that he killed all those innocent lives at the mall. There wasn't a day gone by that I wasn't watching you. I'm not the monster you're looking for Rebecca."

Rebecca knew that being a good profiler she could tell if someone was telling the truth. She looked at Willard and deep down she could tell he was telling her everything. "So why didn't you just come out and tell me all this in the first place?"

"I wanted to tell you Rebecca, I really did. But I was afraid that you wouldn't believe me."

Rebecca was about to say something when she heard a shot from behind. The bullet pierced Willard's chest. Rebecca watched him fall to the floor holding his chest. Rebecca cried out loud. "No!" When she turned around to see who shot him, Adam stood there holding a gun. He dropped the gun on the floor and Rebecca ran up to him. "Adam, why did you shoot him? He was innocent!"

Adam pulled Rebecca towards him and she wrapped her arms around him. Adam started to stroke her hair. "It's going to be alright Rebecca." With his left arm he held her tight against his torso.

Rebecca felt comfortable in Adam's arm as he comforted her. All of a sudden she felt a sharp pain in her gut and as she stood back from Adam she saw that he was holding a bloody knife. She looked down and stumbled on the floor falling nest to Willard. Adam stabbed her in the stomach. "Adam why?" Rebecca couldn't believe the man she loved just stabbed her.

Adam started to laugh in an evil way. "Bitch, you really don't know do you? You should have died at that mall. You should have let Dr. Monteiro kill you that day. But you did let him kill you? No! You let dozens of innocent people die, including my mother." Adam took a step closer to Rebecca. "Do you know what it's like working for an ambulance company being called to a massacre, just to find your mother laying in a pool of blood? You killed the only woman I loved. The only woman I will ever love." He slowly walked towards her and knelt down to be face to face. "It's funny how you really thought I loved you."

Rebecca spat in Adams face. "You mother fucker!"

"Oh, poor little Rebecca." Adam returned the spit in her face. "You're just a fucking slut who sleeps with their co-worker that she only knew for few days." Adam stood back up and Rebecca tried to kick him in the balls. "Good try bitch, but you missed." Adam kept talking. "It was so much fun killing all those people you were making friends with and watching you squirm. You're a cunt Rebecca, and it's going to give me so much pleasure watching your blood gush out of your body after I slice your throat."

Adam lifted his knife to slice her throat, when a gun shot was fired. Adam's head exploded as the bullet exited his head. Brain matter and blood splatted onto Rebecca's face. As Adam fell to the ground, his own knife impaled his chest going right through to the back. Rebecca still in pain from her own stab wound looked up and saw Detective Swanson standing there with his gun in his hand.

Detective Swanson ran up to Rebecca and wiped some of the blood off her face. "Are you alright Rebecca?"

"Yes, I'm alright, besides being stabbed in the stomach. How's Mr. Thorton doing?"

Detective Swanson reached over and looked for a pulse. "He's alive, we better get you two too the hospital."

Detective Swanson phoned in for the ambulance to take both of them to the hospital. The paramedics showed up very quick since the detective called for them ahead of time and they were waiting in the garage. "Thank you for saving my life and hopefully Willard's life."

The detective held her hand. "I took an oath to serve and protect." He walked out of the ambulance. "Rebecca, may I ask you a question?"

"Sure, please ask away."

"How did you know it was Adam?"

"He fit my profile. He was a loner, white male, late 20's early 30's. He also came on too strong to be my friend. I knew something was up when I saw his handwriting on a note that matched the handwriting in blood on the hood of the Jay's car. That's why I called you for back up. I just wish you got there before he stabbed me." Rebecca chuckled. "Damn that hurts." Her laughter hurt her abdomen so she pressed a little harder.

After Rebecca and Willard arrived at the hospital, they both went into emergency surgery. Detective Swanson waited to hear from the doctor. A young man in his 30's walked up to him and removed his surgical mask. "Detective Swanson?"

"Yes, that's me. How are the patients doing?"

The doctor gave him a smile. "They're both lucky to be alive. The knife came inches from cutting a main artery in Rebecca's abdomen and the bullet that pierced Mr. Thorton's chest missed all vital organs. They're both going to recover just fine."

The End!

Made in the USA
Middletown, DE
02 November 2022

13957901R00077